The Old Maid:
The 'Fifties

EDITH WHARTON

THE OLD MAID: THE 'FIFTIES

Introduction by Roxana Robinson

Notes and Publication History by Jennifer Mooney

THE MODERN LIBRARY

NEW YORK

EDITH WHARTON

Edith Wharton, a prolific writer best known as a novelist of manners whose fiction exposed the rigid mores of aristocratic society in a world that has all but vanished, was born Edith Newbold Jones in New York City on January 24, 1862. Both her parents belonged to long-established, socially prominent New York families. Her mother was the former Lucretia Stevens Rhinelander, and her father was George Frederic Jones. (It is said that the expression "keeping up with the Joneses" referred to them.) She was privately educated at home and in Europe by governesses and tutors. "I used to say that I had been taught only two things in my childhood: the modern languages and good manners," she recalled in the compelling memoir *A Backward Glance* (1934). "Now that I have lived to see both those branches of culture dispensed with, I perceive that there are worse systems of education." Her first publication was *Verses* (1878), a book of poems privately printed in Newport when she was sixteen. In later life she brought out two other volumes of poetry, *Artemis to Actaeon and Other Verse* (1909) and *Twelve Poems* (1926), but her verse never succeeded in conveying the emotion of her prose.

In 1885 Edith Jones married Bostonian Edward Robbins Wharton, whom Henry James dubbed "cerebrally compromised Teddy," and over the next decade the couple explored Europe while maintaining residences in New York and Newport. Wharton eventually turned to writing for a measure of fulfillment as she grew dissatisfied with the roles of wife and society matron. In collaboration with architect Ogden Codman she published *The Decoration of Houses* (1897), an influential work on architecture and interior design. Several of her early stories appeared in *Scribner's Magazine*. Three collections, *The Greater Inclination* (1899), *Crucial Instances* (1901), and *The Descent of Man and Other Stories* (1904), display an innate mastery of the short story, which she envisioned as "a shaft driven straight into the heart of human experience." Two novellas, *The Touchstone* (1900) and *Sanctuary* (1903), reveal a talent for psychological realism. Wharton's passion for Italy inspired a first novel, *The Valley of Decision* (1902), as well as *Italian Villas and Their Gardens* (1904) and *Italian Backgrounds* (1905), a series of travel sketches. Her subsequent volumes of travel writing include *A Motor-Flight Through France* (1908) and *In Morocco* (1920).

The publication of *The House of Mirth* in 1905 marked Edith Wharton's coming-of-age as a writer. An immediate bestseller, this brilliant chronicle of upper-class New York society helped secure her reputation as America's foremost woman of letters. By then Wharton was living at "The Mount," a grand home she had built in Lenox, Massachusetts. Over the next years she wrote *Madame de Treymes* (1907), a novella of Jamesian inspiration about young innocents abroad; *The Fruit of the Tree* (1907), a novel of social reform; *The Hermit and the Wild Woman and Other Stories* (1908); and *Tales of Men and Ghosts* (1910), a collection of supernatural thrillers. Then in rapid succession Wharton produced three of her greatest novels: *Ethan Frome* (1911), a tragedy of relinquished passion set against the austere New England countryside; *The Reef* (1912), a richly nuanced story of unrequited love hailed by Henry James as "a triumph of method"; and *The Custom of the Country* (1913), a fierce indictment of the materialism that ruled America in the so-called Gilded Age.

By the time Wharton divorced her husband in 1913 she had settled permanently in France. With the outbreak of World War I she became active in relief work and reported on life at the front in articles for *Scribner's Magazine,* later collected in *Fighting France, from Dunkerque to Belfort* (1915). In 1916 she was decorated with the Cross of the Legion of Honor for her services. During the war years Wharton also wrote *Xingu and Other Stories* (1916); *Summer* (1917), a companion piece to *Ethan Frome;* and *The Marne* (1918), a poignant novel of World War I. *French Ways and Their Meaning,* a collection of essays in praise of her adopted countrymen, came out in 1919.

Wharton was awarded a Pulitzer Prize for *The Age of Innocence* (1920), a masterful portrait of desire and betrayal set in the New York of her youth. Her other acclaimed books of this period include *Old New York* (1924), a quartet of linked novellas that endure as a social history of the city from the 1840s to the 1870s, and *The Writing of Fiction* (1925), a compilation of essays. But critics agree that novels such as *The Glimpses of the Moon* (1922), *A Son at the Front* (1923), *The Mother's Recompense* (1925), *Twilight Sleep* (1927), and *The Children* (1928) signaled a decline in the quality of Wharton's work.

Wharton was elected to the American Academy of Arts and Letters in 1930 and remained highly productive during her final years. Continuing to pursue her lifelong passions for travel, gardening, and interior design, she completed *Hudson River Bracketed* (1929) and *The Gods Arrive* (1932), two interrelated novels that analyze the personality and life of a writer. In addition she turned out five more volumes of short stories: *Here and Beyond* (1926), *Certain People* (1930), *Human Nature* (1933), *The World Over* (1936), and *Ghosts* (1937). Edith Wharton died of a stroke at her villa near Paris on August 11, 1937, and was buried at the Cimetière des Gonards in Versailles. *The Buccaneers,* a novel unfinished at the time of her death, appeared posthumously in 1938.

"At best, there are only three or four American novelists who can be thought of as 'major' and Edith Wharton is one," judged Gore Vidal. "Despite her reputation as being a stuffy *grande dame,* she had always been the most direct and masculine (old sense of the word, naturally) of writers; far more so than her somewhat fussy and hesitant friend Henry James. Spades got called spades in Edith Wharton's novels. . . . Traditionally, Henry James has always been placed slightly higher up the slope of Parnassus than Edith Wharton. But now that the prejudice against the female writer is on the wane, they look to be exactly what they are: giants, equals, the tutelary and benign gods of our American literature."

"Many other writers have attempted to delineate the New York society of old brownstone and new wealth," noted Wharton biographer Louis Auchincloss, "but the reason that Edith Wharton succeeded where almost all of them failed is that, in addition to her great gifts as an artist, her lucidity, her wit, her style, she had a tight grasp of just what this society was made up of. She understood that it was arbitrary, capricious, and inconsistent; she was aware that it did not hesitate to abolish its standards while most loudly proclaiming them. She knew when money could open doors and when it couldn't, when lineage would serve and when it would be merely sneered at. She knew that compromises could be counted on, but that they were rarely made while still considered compromises. She knew her men and women of property, recently or anciently acquired, how they decorated their houses and where they spent their summers. She realized, in short, that the social game was played without rules, and this made her one of the few novelists before Proust who could describe it with profundity. . . . The society of which she wrote was an integral part of the American dream—the American myth—the American illusion."

Contents

THE OLD MAID: THE 'FIFTIES

INTRODUCTION

Roxana Robinson

In her memoir, *A Backward Glance*, Edith Wharton describes a moment in Newport of the 1870s: a group of graceful young women, gathered on a summer lawn for a meeting of the archery club. The bright sun, the green space, the sparkling sea air set off these maids, who wear white "floating silks or muslins, with their wide leghorn hats, and heavy veils flung back only at the moment of aiming."

Their faces are completely hidden. The heavy veils are wrapped around their hats, stretched over their features, tucked carefully around their necks. This was for protection, to keep the translucent skin from being raked by sunlight or roughened by sea-wind. In that world, beauty was paramount, and "No grace," wrote Wharton, "was rated as high as 'a complexion.' It is hard to picture nowadays the shell-like transparence, the luminous red-and-white of those young cheeks untouched by paint or powder, in which the blood came and went like the lights of an aurora. Beauty was unthinkable without 'a complexion,' and to defend that treasure against sun and wind ... veils as thick as curtains ... were habitually worn. It must have been very uncomfortable to the wearers, who could hardly see or breathe: but even to my childish eyes the effect was dazzling when the curtain was drawn, and young beauty shone forth."

Striking as is this image of transparency and beauty, even more so is the notion of cherishing and protection implied by the closely veiled faces: these young women were jewels. Their loveliness—source of their attraction, sign of their worth—was carefully guarded. Their luminous, glowing skin was masked against the burning sunlight, their lissome forms were blurred by floating silks, even their own vision was obscured by close-woven shields. Exposure meant risk. Chaperoned, attended, they lived under close familial scrutiny during the perilous age of marriageability, revealed only, briefly, during "the moment of aiming." When the shaft had struck its mark, the bridegroom stepped forward with the proprietary right to lift the veil. Until then, these closely swathed and virginal figures, emblems of value and virtue in Wharton's "Old New York," led a chaste and cloistered life. They were governed by strict social codes, obedient to fixed and immutable laws.

And yet . . . and yet. Is it ever possible to live according to fixed and immutable laws? Were there moments in which those veils were privately loosened, secretly lifted?

———

Edith Jones Wharton was born in 1862 into the fashionable inner circles of New York, a fact that would reverberate throughout her fiction. Providing both setting and drama, the world of the well-bred was portrayed in endless variations within her work. This was a small, tribal society with a strict caste system, governed by copious and inflexible laws. These addressed every sort of comportment, from the paying of social calls to the arbitration of morality. Obedience to them was a requisite for membership in the community; breaking them meant the risk of expulsion.

Edith Wharton obeyed the rules. She married a young man of good family, joined the "young married set" in New York, and spent summers in Newport. Her life, however, was one of increasing isolation, both emotional and intellectual: her husband was unfaithful and unstable, and her circles excluded writers. After twenty-eight years of marriage, Wharton broke the rules, divorcing her husband. In 1913 she moved to France, where she spent the rest of her life. Paris, more tolerant and sophisticated than New York, welcomed her into the rich, vital mix of the salon—despite her being female, intellectual, and divorced.

Though Wharton had left old New York, it was deeply engrained within her. She had broken its rules but she respected their potency. Her perceptions of this world would change, but it would remain at the center of her experience, and it would be central to her best work.

In 1905, still married, still in New York, Wharton published *The House of Mirth*. In this elegant tragedy, the beautiful, impecunious Lily Bart is unable to survive within the heartless and superficial world of New York Society. Though we pity Lily, we cannot imagine her happiness in this deadly, vapid place, with its rigid rules, idle pastimes, and disloyal, adulterous friends. The social code here seems punitive and empty—form without substance.

The Custom of the Country (1913) addressed the subversive issue of divorce—fresh in Wharton's mind. The shrewd adventuress Undine Spragg trades her troth repeatedly for advancement. Deftly she climbs the social ladder, grasping, with the aid of accommodating husbands, at ever higher prizes. The old world here is elegant, faded, and moribund, its laws powerless over someone so vulgar and materialistic, who values neither tradition nor family. The new world, that of the arriviste, is worse: glittering, cold, and dreadful.

At the end of World War I, Wharton, in her late fifties, was deeply affected by the grief that blanketed her adopted country. The brilliant world she had loved had vanished; she felt *dépaysée*. She told a friend sadly, *"Je me cherche, et je ne me trouve pas."* Nineteenth-century America was gone; twentieth-century America was alien. "All that I thought American in a true sense is gone, and I see nothing but vain-glory, crassness and a total ignorance . . . ," she wrote. She began to reconsider the old, lost world. What had seemed once petty and insular now seemed valuable and dignified; the rules, she saw, had been founded on moral principle. "I am steeping myself in the nineteenth century," she wrote, ". . . such a blessed refuge from the turmoil and mediocrity of today—like taking sanctuary in a mighty temple."

In 1919–1920, Wharton wrote *The Age of Innocence*, set in the 1870s. This exquisite, elegiac work, with its themes of love and renunciation, is her most powerful tribute to that lost world. Here the strict social codes are part of a larger moral imperative, one that protects the community at the expense of the individual. Ellen Olenska and Newland Archer sacrifice their own happiness for that of others, nobly upholding an ideal of honor and the greater good.

In 1921, still mining the rich vein of the past, Wharton began a quartet of novellas, titled collectively *Old New York*. Each dealt with a nineteenth-century decade: *False Dawn: The 'Forties; The Old Maid: The 'Fifties; The Spark: The 'Sixties;* and *New Year's Day: The 'Seventies*. Published in separate volumes, in 1924, they were declared by *The New York Times* to be among Wharton's best work. *The Old Maid* was called "one of the most beautiful stories in the whole range of American literature." It sold three times as well as the others, though periodicals had rejected it as "too unpleasant."

The Old Maid, written in 1921, is indeed beautiful in its construction, and its subject is indeed unpleasant. Like Wharton's bleak tale of retribution, *Ethan Frome*, this delivers truths we might rather not know. *The Old Maid*, however, is more complex and more assured than the earlier work. The execution is brilliant and the construction nearly flawless: Wharton weaves a golden, fine-meshed net about her characters with inexorable precision.

The Old Maid is set in a staid, unimaginative society, embodied by the stolid and conventional Ralston family, "of middle-class English stock." They are industrious, decent, and deeply cautious; heroism is seen as too risky. Their sensibility provides the moral backdrop to the story.

The narrative centers on two women. As in much of Wharton's fiction, the men play minor roles. Few male characters in her work—or her life—were both powerful and principled, and here the men are largely passive or absent. The protagonists are Delia and Charlotte, Lovell cousins. Delia, the beauty, from a comfortable background, has married steady Jim Ralston. She has two pretty children and a pretty bedroom in a pretty house on Gramercy Park. She is happy being a Ralston, though she remembers the man she did not marry: impetuous Clement Spender, who chose art in Rome over law in New York.

Charlotte, by contrast, is a poor Lovell, and plain, with eyes and hair a pale common brown. Her father died young, and her widowed mother was unable to help her enter Society. Charlotte languished in the marriage-market, then tuberculosis flushed her cheek with its sinister stain. But now Charlotte is healthy again, and engaged to Joe Ralston. Her face is nearly pretty; even her hair seems darker. She has sailed into safe harbor.

The scene is set for complications: Delia admires herself in her mirror as Charlotte arrives, distraught, and throws herself on Delia's love seat. The complications unfold like the petals of an intricate flower. Issues emerge: secrecy, the violation of codes. Betrayal. Deception. Jealousy, compassion, rage. Retribution, love. The unthinkable: sexuality.

In her photographs, Edith Wharton is so straight-backed, so correct. Her hair is so impeccably smooth, her wide pearl choker so high and tight. Her demeanor shows such formality and restraint. And her writing is as elegant and formal as her demeanor: how can this decorous person have such thoughts? How can these polished, mannerly sentences describe such improprieties? But they do: Wharton's work is full of the wide dark tide of sexuality, its roiling luxuriance, its sweet potency.

Like all novelists, Wharton drew on her own experience, and there are parallels between her own mother, Lucretia, and that of Charlotte. Lucretia was "a poor Rhinelander" whose widowed mother gave her little help. Both women wore hand-me-down slippers to their coming-out balls; both had grandmothers with yellow coaches and fringed hammer-cloths. But there the stories diverged: Lucretia married a man of good family, put poverty behind her, and led a decorous, conventional life. Or did they diverge completely? Was there a connecting thread? A scarlet one?

Edith's birth—the last in the family—must have been something of a surprise: there were twelve long years between herself and her closest brother. It was widely rumored that the reason for this was Edith's paternity—that her father was not Frederic Jones, but the young English tutor living with the family, teaching Edith's brothers. Edith was said to resemble the young man to a shocking degree. R.W.B. Lewis, Wharton's biographer, thinks the rumors were unfounded, but what is known to be true is that Edith was aware of them. She understood that such a thing could happen in her small, strictly controlled world—even in her family's small, strictly controlled household. She knew the unthinkable was possible.

Sexual knowledge is the fulcrum on which *The Old Maid* turns, as its name suggests. The knowledge was charged, forbidden, secret. The young women of this era were to arrive at the altar virginal and untouched, unsullied even by information. The chaste Delia, on her wedding night, was mystified but obedient, yielding to her husband's incomprehensible demands.

Charlotte's sexual initiation was different. Poor and plain, she did not attract the attentions of the man she loved. Without attentive parents, she lacked guardianship; unchaperoned, she yielded to the importunate advances of a man she loves but who, she knows, does not love her, and, worse, will not marry her. The illicit scene is thrillingly imagined by Delia: the dark parlor, the swathed chandelier; the infirm grandmother and servants asleep on the upper floors; the silent lovers in the moonlight. It is a scene infinitely more urgent and compelling than Delia's modest, confused initiation in the big white bed. Because of this secret passage, poor plain Charlotte is suddenly revealed as more exotic, more dangerous and glamorous; more worldly and knowing than the matronly, domestic Delia.

There is no greater social crime, no greater transgression of the codes, than for a girl of good breeding to have an illegitimate child. The laws are implacable; retribution inescapable. Charlotte must be punished for her illicit knowledge, and the instrument of the law, its enforcer, is her chaste and decorous cousin. It is Delia who upholds the code of the Ralstons, who undertakes to protect the community—and not simply on moral grounds. Her attitude is marvelously complicated, for Delia's thick braid of righteousness contains not only a bright strand of compassion—for wouldn't it be possible somehow to salvage Charlotte's happiness?—but also a vivid strand of envy. Hasn't her poorer, plainer cousin taken something that Delia believed was hers? The lover, Delia learns, is Clement Spender, and didn't he belong to her? This secret sense of betrayal turns Delia high-handed, imperious, and relentless. Her personal outrage feeds her moral indignation, and, like an avenging deity, Delia the Chaste metes out Charlotte's punishment.

There are connections between *The Old Maid* and *The Age of Innocence*. Ellen was originally named Clementina Olenska. The two lovers—Ellen and Newland—were to consummate their love, before parting forever. But the most significant connection lies in the functioning of the moral code. In both stories, the laws of the community must be served absolutely, protecting the institutions—marriage, the family, the legitimacy of bloodline—at great and painful cost to the individual.

Charlotte must be punished for her knowledge, and Delia rewarded for her chastity. Charlotte relinquishes all public maternal rights and privileges in exchange for remaining within the community. Her persona is transmuted from the beloved one of the Virgin—rich with the possibilities of the future—to the despised one of the Old Maid—symbol of emotional and biological barrenness. The law-abiding Delia is given infinite power over her sinful cousin. Both of them adore Charlotte's beautiful child, Tina, who has a charged fascination for them. Tina represents the life each woman might have had, and for which each secretly yearns. As the story's knots twist tighter and tighter, the issue of illicit sexual knowledge arises again, this time over the risk to Tina. Charlotte, fiercely protective, prepares boldly to leave the community, taking Tina elsewhere to seek a legitimate, more modest life. Delia, desperate to keep Tina, exquisitely cruel, accuses Charlotte of sacrificing her daughter to her own "desire for mastery."

Each woman loves the child; each wants to claim motherhood. Each uses the other for the child's good. But power lies with Delia the Chaste, and with each excruciating turn of the plot, Charlotte loses more of her maternal connection. With each new binding twist, Wharton imposes the lessons of this forbidden knowledge, the iron inexorability of the law that governs it.

Charlotte's sacrifice has, however, achieved its goal; these laws are strict but just. Charlotte has given up a mother's role to become an object of charity, sacrificing her life for her daughter's future. But she has remained within the community, and Tina has been accepted. The child has been cherished, given a name and a dowry. On the eve of her wedding (to a young man of good family) Tina is legitimate, modestly affluent—and still innocent.

In the final conflict, the rival mothers clash over Tina's prenuptial instruction. The old issues emerge: Charlotte's deep and endless wound, Delia's struggle between envy and compassion. Charlotte yields; then Delia foregoes the privilege. The bride will still remain innocent, unaware of sexual knowledge or its cost. The struggle is over: Charlotte has yielded the last scrap of motherhood to Delia. The law has been obeyed, the price paid, and the punishment is complete.

Delia the Chaste, the avenger, satisfied by Charlotte's expiation, now relents. Revealing her compassionate aspect, Delia bestows a final blessing on both mother and daughter—now that she has, victorious, separated them forever.

———

ROXANA ROBINSON is the author of two previous novels, a biography of Georgia O'Keeffe, and two short-story collections. She has received fellowships from the Guggenheim Foundation, the National Endowment for the Arts, and the MacDowell Colony. Robinson's fiction has appeared in *Best American Short Stories*, *The Atlantic*, *The New Yorker*, *Harper's*, and *Vogue*. She lives in New York City and Westchester County, New York.

PUBLICATION HISTORY

Jennifer Mooney

Scribner's, Harper's, Atlantic Monthly, Saturday Evening Post, Ladies' Home Journal. The list of magazines in which Edith Wharton's work was published reads like a directory of the nineteenth and early twentieth centuries' most prestigious literary and women's periodicals. Wharton's involvement with periodical publication, in fact, spanned her entire career, from the appearance of her earliest travel essays, poems, and fiction in *Scribner's* (1889) to the posthumous printing of the autobiographical article "A Little Girl's New York" in *Harper's* (1938). None of her works, however, prompted upon submission the same measure of response as did her novella *The Old Maid.*

This novella, which recounts the unique relationship between cousins Delia Ralston and Charlotte Lovell as they care jointly for the latter's illegitimate child, was written, according to Wharton biographer R.W.B. Lewis, "in the last months of 1921" (3). As Lewis notes, earlier that year, Wharton had intended to publish in one volume—tentatively titled *Among the Mingotts*—two novellas about life in nineteenth-century New York that would continue her exploration of the social milieu begun a year earlier in *The Age of Innocence* (435). Although her plans for the edition subsequently

changed, with *The Old Maid,* Wharton completed the first install-
ment of what would eventually become the tetralogy *Old New York.*

First for *The Old Maid,* however, came submission for serial
publication. Wharton had published with *Ladies' Home Journal* previously, but when her newest story came across his desk, the magazine's editor rejected it, noting, "It's a bit too vigorous for us"
(Lewis, 435).[1] *Metropolitan* magazine likewise passed on the novella,
declaring it to be powerful but "simply too unpleasant" (Lewis, 436).
Wharton's response was immediate and ironic. To her favorite pub-
lisher at Appleton, Rutger Bleecker Jewett (1867–1935), she writes
on May 23, "Have the readers of the Metropolitan never read 'The
Scarlet Letter' or 'Adam Bede' to mention only the two first classics
that come to my mind? And how about my own 'Summer'?" (*Letters,*
443).[2] The sting, however, was tempered by some good news. In a
June 7, 1921, letter to her friend Bernard Berenson (1865–1959),
the Lithuanian-born art critic and author, Wharton writes of both
the negative and the decidedly positive:

> Apparently every self-respecting American magazine has refused 'The
> Old Maid' on the ground of immorality! I suppose one of the periodi-
> cal (in both senses) waves of pruriency has set in.—But meanwhile Co-
> lumbia has awarded me the—Pulitzer!!—$1000—prize for the best
> novel of the year. (*Letters,* 441–42).

With the power of the Pulitzer behind Wharton, *The Old Maid*
was now deemed worth the risk. In 1921, Appleton was able to place
the story with *The Red Book Magazine* (now simply *Redbook*), where it
ran in three issues: February, March, and April 1922 (Wright, 212).
For it, Wharton earned $2,250 (Lewis, 436). A year later, in July and
August 1923, the magazine would publish *New Year's Day.*

In 1924, Appleton published *Old New York* as a boxed set. It con-
sisted of four novellas: *The Old Maid, New Year's Day, False Dawn*
(which appeared in *Ladies' Home Journal* in 1923), and *The Spark*
(*Ladies' Home Journal,* 1924). Endpiece illustrations were added by
Edward Caswell (Lewis, 459). In his review of the volume in *The
New York Times,* Lloyd Morris singled out *The Old Maid* for praise,

calling it "one of the most beautiful stories in the whole range of American literature" (reprinted in Lewis, 459). Readers must have agreed with his assessment. As Lewis notes, *The Old Maid* sold "three times more than any of the other individual volumes" (459).

Since then, *The Old Maid* has been reprinted in a number of collections and, according to Vito Brenni, has been translated numerous times, appearing, for example, as *Eu Soube Amar* (in Brazil) and *La Solterona* (in Spain).

The novella has also been adapted as a stage play and as a Hollywood film. In 1935, Zoe Akins's stage adaptation—which featured Judith Anderson and Helen Menken—played for 305 dates at the Empire Theatre (Marshall and Wright, 293). Subsequently, it won a Pulitzer Prize (1935), and the dramatization has been revived numerous times. In 1939, Casey Robinson produced a screenplay that drew on both Wharton's novella and Akins's play. The period of the film, starring Bette Davis (as Charlotte) and Miriam Hopkins, was shifted to the Civil War (Marshall). This alteration occurred, according to Sarah Bird Wright, "to take advantage of *Gone with the Wind* mania" (191). Although the film won no awards, it was one of several melodramas that Davis and Hopkins made together.

For a story initially rejected by some publishers as too controversial—too *unpleasant,* too *vigorous*—*The Old Maid* remains a vital contribution to the Wharton oeuvre. Its representation of the individual spirit constrained by a rigid, totem-ridden (to borrow Wharton's phrase) society holds true no matter in which media—print, film, stage, even e-text—it appears.

NOTES

1. *Ladies' Home Journal* had previously published two Wharton articles: "Is There a New Frenchwoman?" (1917) and its revision, "The New Frenchwoman" (1919).
2. In this story, published by Appleton in 1917, another story of illegitimacy is told: Charity Royall becomes pregnant by the socially ambitious Lucius Harney, is abandoned, and is then rescued by marriage with the man who had previously adopted her.

WORKS CITED AND CONSULTED

Brenni, Vito. *Edith Wharton: A Bibliography.* Morgantown: West Virginia University Library, 1966.

Lewis, R.W.B. *Edith Wharton: A Biography.* New York: Harper & Row, 1975.

———and Nancy Lewis, eds. *The Letters of Edith Wharton.* New York: Scribner's, 1988.

Marshall, Scott. "Edith Wharton on Film and Television: A Filmography."

———and Sarah Bird Wright. "Theatrical Adaptations of Edith Wharton's Works." *Edith Wharton: A to Z. Sarah Bird Wright.* New York: Facts on File, 1998. 292–294.

Wright, Sarah Bird. *Edith Wharton A to Z: The Essential Guide to the Life and Work.* New York: Facts on File, 1998.

A Note on the Text

The Old Maid originally appeared in serial form in *The Red Book Magazine* from February to April of 1922, the texts of which this edition is set from. Later, in 1924, Appleton published the novella, along with three others, in a volume entitled *Old New York,* for which *The Old Maid* was heavily edited. Unfortunately, it cannot be ascertained whether Wharton participated in these numerous changes. All changes made to the 1924 book edition are noted and explained.

THE OLD MAID:
THE 'FIFTIES

CHAPTER I

In the old New York of the 'thirties[1] a few families ruled, in simplicity and affluence. Of these were the Ralstons. The sturdy English and the rubicund and heavier Dutch had mingled to produce a prosperous, prudent and yet lavish society. To "do things handsomely" had always been a fundamental principle in this cautious world, built up on the fortunes of bankers, India merchants, shipbuilders, and shipchandlers.[2] Those well-fed, slow-moving people, who seemed irritable and dyspeptic to European eyes only because the caprices of the climate had stripped them of superfluous flesh, and strung their nerves a little tighter, lived in a genteel monotony of which the surface was never stirred by the dumb dramas now and then enacted underground. Sensitive souls in those days were like muted keyboards, on which Fate played without a sound.[3]

In this compact society, built of solidly welded blocks, one of the largest areas was filled by the Ralstons and their ramifications. The Ralstons were of middle-class English stock. They had not come to the colonies to die for a creed but to live for a bank-account.[4] The result had been beyond their hopes, and their religion was tinged by their success. An edulcorated Church of England[5] which, under the conciliatory name of the "Episcopal Church of the United States of

America," left out the coarser allusions in the Marriage Service, slid over the comminatory passages in the Athanasian Creed,[6] and thought it more respectful to say "Our Father *who*" than *"which"* in the Lord's Prayer, was exactly suited to the spirit of compromise whereon the Ralstons had built themselves up. There was in all the tribe the same instinctive recoil from new religions as from unaccounted-for people. Institutional to the core, they represented the conservative element that holds new societies together as sea-plants[7] bind the seashore.

Compared with the Ralstons, even such traditionalists as the Lovells, the Halseys or the Vandergraves appeared careless, indifferent to money, almost reckless in their impulses and indecisions. Old John Frederick Ralston, the stout founder of the race, had perceived the difference, and emphasized it to his son, Frederick John, in whom he had scented a faint leaning toward the untried and unprofitable.

"You let the Lannings and the Dagonets and the Spenders take risks and fly kites.[8] It's the county-family blood in 'em: we've nothing to do with that. Look how they're petering out already—the men, I mean. Let your boys marry their girls, if you like (they're wholesome and handsome); though I'd sooner see my grandsons take a Lovell or a Vandergrave, than any of our own kind. But don't let your sons go mooning around with their young fellows, horse-racing, and running down south to those damned springs,[9] and gambling at New Orleans, and all the rest of it. That's how you'll build up the family, and keep the weather out. The way we've always done it."[10]

Frederick John listened, obeyed, married a Halsey, and passively followed in his father's steps. He belonged to the cautious generation of New York gentlemen who revered Hamilton and served Jefferson,[11] who longed to lay out New York like Washington, and who laid it out instead like a gridiron, lest they should be thought "undemocratic"[12] by people they secretly looked down upon. Shopkeepers to the marrow, they put in their windows the wares there was most demand for, keeping their private opinions for the back-shop, where, through lack of use, they gradually lost substance and color.[13]

The present generation of Ralstons had nothing left in the way of convictions save an acute sense of honor in private and business matters; on the life of the community and the state they took their daily views from the newspapers, and the newspapers they already despised. They themselves had done little to shape the destiny of their country, except to finance the Cause[14] when it had become safe to do so. They were related to many of the great men who had built the Republic; but no Ralston had so far committed himself as to be great. As old John Frederick said, it was safer to be satisfied with three per cent: they regarded heroism as a form of gambling. Yet by merely being so numerous and so similar they had come to have a weight in the community. People said, "The Ralstons," when they wished to invoke a precedent. This attribution of authority had gradually convinced the third generation of its collective importance; and the fourth, to which Delia Ralston's husband belonged, had the ease and simplicity of a ruling class.[15]

Within the limits of their universal caution, the Ralstons fulfilled their obligations as rich and respected citizens. They figured on the boards of all the old-established charities,[16] gave handsomely to thriving institutions, had the best cooks in New York, and when they traveled abroad ordered statuary of the American sculptors in Rome whose reputation was already made.[17] The first Ralston who had brought home a statue had been regarded as a wild fellow; but when it became known that the sculptor had executed several orders for the British aristocracy, it was felt in the family that this too was a three-per-cent investment.[18]

Two marriages with the Dutch Vandergraves had consolidated these qualities of thrift and handsome living, and the carefully built-up Ralston character was now so congenital that Delia Ralston sometimes asked herself whether, were she to turn her little boy loose in a wilderness, he would not create a small New York there, and be on all its boards of directors.

Delia Lovell had married James Ralston at twenty. The marriage, which had taken place in the month of September, 1840, had been solemnized, as was then the custom, in the drawing-room of the bride's country home,[19] at what is now the corner of Avenue A and Ninety-first Street, overlooking the Sound. Thence her husband had driven her (in Grandmamma Lovell's canary-colored coach with a fringed hammer-cloth),[20] through spreading suburbs and untidy elm-shaded streets, to one of the new houses in Gramercy Park,[21] which the pioneers of the younger set were just beginning to affect; and there, at five-and-twenty, she was established, the mother of two children, the possessor of a generous allowance of pin-money,[22] and, by common consent, one of the handsomest and most popular "young matrons" (as they were called) of her day.

She was thinking placidly and gratefully of these things as she sat one day in her handsome bedroom in Gramercy Park. She was too near to the primitive Ralstons to have as clear a view of them as, for instance, the son in question might one day command: she lived under them as unthinkingly as one lives under the laws of one's country. Yet that tremor in her of the muted keyboard, that secret questioning which sometimes beat in her like wings, would now and then so divide her from them that for a fleeting moment she could survey them in their relation to other things. The moment was always fleeting: she dropped back from it quickly, breathless and a little pale, to her children, her housekeeping, her new dresses and her kindly Jim.[23]

She thought of him today with a smile of tenderness, remembering how he had told her to spare no expense on her new bonnet. Though she was twenty-five, and twice a mother, her image was still surprisingly fresh. The plumpness then thought seemly in a young matron stretched the gray silk across her bosom, and caused her heavy gold watch-chain—after it left the anchorage of the brooch of St. Peter's in mosaic that fastened her low-cut Cluny collar[24]—to dangle perilously in the void, above a tiny waist buckled into a velvet waist-band. But the shoulders above sloped youthfully under her Cashmere scarf,[25] and every movement was as quick as a girl's.[26]

—

Mrs. Ralston[27] approvingly examined the rosy-cheeked oval set in the blonde ruffles of the bonnet on which, in compliance with her husband's instructions, she had spared no expense. It was a cabriolet[28] of white velvet tied with wide satin ribbons and plumed with a crystal-spangled marabou[29]—a wedding bonnet ordered for the marriage of her cousin, Charlotte Lovell, which was to take place that week at St. Mark's-in-the-Bouwerie.[30] Charlotte was making a match exactly like Delia's own: marrying a Ralston, of the Waverley Place[31] branch, than which nothing could be safer, sounder or more—well, usual. Delia did not know why the word had occurred to her, for it could hardly be postulated, even of the young women of her own narrow clan, that they "usually" married Ralstons; but the soundness, safeness, suitability of the arrangement, did make it typical of the kind of alliance which a nice girl in the nicest set would serenely and blushfully[32] forecast for herself.

Yes—and afterward?

Well—what? And what did this new question mean? Afterward; why, of course, there was the startled, unprepared surrender to the incomprehensible exigencies of the young man to whom one had at most accorded a rosy cheek in return for an engagement ring; there was the large double bed; the terror of seeing him shaving calmly the next morning, in his shirt-sleeves, through the dressing-room door; the evasions, insinuations, resigned smiles and Bible texts of one's Mamma; the reminder of the phrase "to obey" in the glittering blur of the Marriage Service: a week or a month of flushed distress, confusion, embarrassed pleasure; then the growth of habit, the insidious lulling of the matter-of-course, dreamless double slumbers in the big white bed, early-morning discussions and consultations through that dressing-room door which had once seemed to open into a fiery pit scorching the brow of innocence.[33]

And then, the babies: the babies who were supposed to "make up for everything," and didn't—though they were such darlings, and one had no definite notion as to what it was that one had missed, and that they were to make up for.

Yes: Charlotte's fate would be just like hers. Joe Ralston was so like his second cousin Jim (Delia's James), that Delia could see no reason why life in the squat brick house in Waverley Place should not exactly resemble life in the tall brownstone house in Gramercy Park. Only Charlotte's bedroom would certainly not be as pretty as hers.[34]

———

She glanced complacently at the French wall-paper that reproduced a watered silk, with a "valanced" border and tassels between the loops. The mahogany bedstead, covered with a white embroidered counterpane,[35] was symmetrically reflected in the mirror of the wardrobe that matched it. Colored lithographs of the "Four Seasons" by Leopold Robert[36] surmounted groups of family daguerruotypes[37] in deeply recessed gilt frames. The ormolu clock[38] represented a shepherdess sitting on a fallen trunk, a basket of flowers at her feet. A shepherd, stealing up, surprised her with a kiss, while her little dog barked at him from a clump of roses. One knew the profession of the lovers by their crooks and the shape of their hats. This frivolous timepiece had been a wedding-gift from Delia's aunt, Mrs. Manson Mingott,[39] a dashing widow who lived in Paris and was received at the Tuileries.[40] It had been intrusted by her to young Clement Spender, who had come back from Italy for a short holiday just after Delia's marriage: the marriage which might never have been, if Clem Spender could have supported a wife, or had consented to give up painting and Rome for New York and the law. The young man (who looked, already, so odd and foreign and sarcastic) had laughingly assured the bride that her aunt's gift was "the newest thing in the Palais Royal;" and the family, who admired Mrs. Manson Mingott's taste, though they disapproved of her "foreignness," had criticized Delia's putting the clock in her bedroom instead of displaying it on the drawing-room mantel. But she liked, when she woke in the morning, to see the bold shepherd stealing his kiss.[41]

Charlotte would certainly not have such a pretty clock in her bedroom; but then, she had not been used to pretty things. Her father, who had died at thirty of lung-fever,[42] was one of the "poor Lovells." His widow, burdened with a young family, and living all the year round "up the River,"[43] could not do much for her eldest girl; and Charlotte had entered society in her mother's turned garments,[44] and shod with satin sandals handed down from a defunct great-aunt who had "opened a ball"[45] with General Washington. The old-fashioned Ralston furniture, which Delia already saw herself gradually banishing, would seem sumptuous to Chatty; very likely she would think Delia's gay French timepiece somewhat frivolous, or even "not quite nice." Poor Charlotte had become so serious, so prudish almost, since she had given up balls and taken to visiting the poor! Delia remembered, with ever-recurring wonder, the abrupt change in her: the precise moment at which it had been privately agreed in the family that, after all, Charlotte Lovell was going to be an old maid.[46]

They had not thought so when she came out. Though her mother could not afford to give her more than one new tarlatan[47] dress, and though nearly everything in her appearance was regrettable, from the too bright red of her hair to the too pale brown of her eyes,—not to mention the rounds of brick-rose on her cheekbones, which almost (preposterous thought!) made her look as if she painted,[48]—yet these defects were redeemed by a slim waist, a light foot and a gay laugh; and when her hair was well oiled[49] and brushed for an evening party, so that it looked almost brown, and lay smoothly along her delicate cheeks, under a wreath of red[50] and white camellias, several eligible young men (Joe Ralston among them) were known to have called her pretty.[51]

———

Then came her illness. She caught cold on a moonlight sleighing-party; the brick-rose circles deepened, and she began to cough. There was a report that she was "going like her father," and she was hurried off to a remote village in Georgia, where she lived alone for a year with an old family governess. When she came back, every one felt at once that there was a change in her. She was pale, and thinner than ever, but with an exquisitely transparent cheek, darker eyes and redder hair; and the oddness of her appearance was increased by plain dresses of Quakerish cut.[52] She had left off trinkets and watch-chains, always wore the same gray cloak and small close bonnet, and displayed a sudden zeal for visiting the poor. The family explained that during her year in the South she had been shocked by the hopeless degradation of the "poor whites" and their children, and that this revelation of misery had made it impossible for her to return to the light-hearted life of her contemporaries. Everyone agreed, with an exchange of significant glances, that this unnatural state of mind would "pass off in time;" and meanwhile old Mrs. Lovell, Chatty's grandmother, who understood her perhaps better than the others, gave her a little money for her paupers, and lent her a room in the Lovell stables (at the back of the old Mercer Street house) where she gathered about her, in what would afterward have been called a "day-nursery,"[53] some of the poor children of the neighborhood.[54]

There was even, among them, the baby girl whose origin had excited such intense curiosity in the neighborhood two or three years earlier, when a veiled lady in handsome clothes had brought it to the hovel of Cyrus Washington, the negro handy-man whose wife Jessamine took in Dr. Lanskell's washing. Dr. Lanskell was the chief practitioner of the day, and presumably versed in the secret history of every household from the Battery[55] to Union Square; but though beset by inquisitive patients, he had invariably declared himself unable to identify Jessamine's "veiled lady," or to hazard a guess as to the origin of the hundred-dollar bill pinned to the baby's cloak.[56]

The hundred dollars were never renewed; the lady never reappeared; but the baby lived healthily and happily with Jessamine's pickaninnies,[57] and as soon as it could toddle, was brought to Chatty Lovell's day nursery, where it appeared (like its fellow-paupers) in little garments cut down from her old dresses, and socks knitted by her untiring hands. Delia, absorbed in her own babies, had nevertheless dropped in once or twice at the nursery, and had come away wishing that Chatty's maternal instinct might find its normal outlet in marriage and motherhood. The married cousin confusedly felt that her own affection for her handsome children was a mild and measured sentiment compared with Chatty's fierce passion for the plebeian waifs in Grandmamma Lovell's stable.[58]

And then, to the general surprise, Charlotte Lovell engaged herself to Joe Ralston. It was known that Joe had "admired her" the year she came out. She was a graceful dancer, and Joe, who was tall and nimble, had footed it with her through many a reel and Schottisch.[59] By the end of the winter all the match-makers were predicting that something would come of it; but when Delia playfully sounded her cousin, the girl's evasive answer and burning brow seemed to imply that her suitor had changed his mind, and no more questions had been asked. Now it became evident that there had, in fact, been an old romance, probably followed by that exciting incident, a "misunderstanding;" but at last all was well, and the bells of St. Mark's were about to ring in happier days for Charlotte. "Ah, when she has her first baby," the Ralston mothers chorused.[60]

—

"Chatty!" Delia exclaimed, pushing back her chair as she saw her cousin's image reflected in the glass over her shoulder.

Charlotte Lovell had paused in the doorway. "They told me you were here—so I ran up."

"Of course, darling. How handsome you do look in your poplin![61] I always said you needed rich materials. I'm so thankful to see you out of brown cashmere."[62]

Delia lifted her hands, and raising the white bonnet from her dark polished head, shook it so that the crystals glittered.[63]

"I hope you like it? It's for your wedding," she laughed.

Charlotte Lovell stood motionless. In her mother's old dove-colored poplin, freshly banded with rows of crimson velvet ribbon, an ermine tippet[64] crossed on her bosom, and a new beaver bonnet with a falling feather, she had already something of the assurance and majesty of a married woman.

"And you know your hair *is* darker,[65] darling." Delia added, still hopefully surveying her.

"Darker? It's gray," Charlotte broke out in her deep voice, pushing back one of the pomaded bands that framed her face, and showing a white lock on her temple. "You needn't save up your bonnet. I'm not going to be married," she added harshly, with a smile that showed her teeth in a fleeting glare.[66]

Delia had just enough presence of mind to lay down the white bonnet, marabou up,[67] before she flung herself on her cousin.

"Not going to be married? Charlotte, are you perfectly crazy?"

"Why is it crazy to do what I think right?"

"But people said you were going to marry him the year you came out. And no one understood what happened then. And now—how can it possibly be right? You simply *can't*!" Delia incoherently summed up.[68]

"Oh—people!" said Charlotte wearily.[69]

Her married cousin looked at her with a start. Something thrilled in her voice that Delia had never heard in it, or in any other human voice, before. Its echo seemed to set their familiar world rocking, and the Axminster carpet[70] actually heaved under Delia's shrinking slippers.[71]

———

Charlotte stood staring ahead of her with strained lids. In the pale brown of her eyes Delia noticed the green specks that floated there when she was angry or excited.

"Charlotte—where on earth have you come from?" she cried,[72] drawing the girl down to the sofa.

"Come from?"

"Yes. You look as if you'd seen a ghost—an army of ghosts."

The same snarling smile drew up Charlotte's lip. "I've seen Joe," she said.

"Well? . . . Oh, Chatty." Delia cried, abruptly illuminated, "you don't mean to say that you're going to let any little thing in Joe's past—not that I've ever heard the least hint, never. But if there were—" She drew a deep breath, and bravely proceeded to extremities. "Even if you've heard that he's been—that he's had a child—of course he would have provided for it before—"[73]

The girl shook her head. "I know; you needn't go on. 'Men will be men;'[74] but it's not that."

"Tell me what it is."

Charlotte Lovell looked about the sunny, prosperous room[75] as if it were the image of her world, and that world were a prison she must break out of. She lowered her head. "I want—to get away," she panted.

"Get away? From Joe?"

"From his ideas—the Ralston ideas."

Delia bridled—after all, she was a Ralston! "The Ralston ideas? I haven't found them—so unbearably unpleasant to live with," she smiled a little tartly.

"No. But it was different with you: they didn't ask you to give up things."

"What things?" What in the world, Delia wondered, had poor Charlotte, that anyone could want her to give up?[76] She had always been in the position of taking rather than of having to surrender. "Can't you explain to me, dear?" Delia urged.

"My poor children—he says I'm to give them up," cried the girl in a stricken whisper.

"Give them up? Give up helping them?"

"Seeing them—looking after them. Give them up altogether. He got his mother to explain to me. After—after we have children, he's afraid—afraid our children might catch things. . . . He'll give me money, of course, to pay some one—a hired person to look after them. He thought that handsome," Charlotte broke out in a sob. She flung off her bonnet and smothered her weeping in the cushions.[77]

———

Delia sat perplexed. Of all unforeseen complications this was surely the least imaginable. And with all the acquired Ralston that was in her she could not help seeing the force of Joe's objection, could almost find herself agreeing with him. No one in New York had forgotten the death of the poor Henry van der Luydens' only child, from small-pox[78] caught at the circus to which an unprincipled nurse had surreptitiously taken him. After that warning,[79] parents felt justified in every precaution against contagion. And poor people were so ignorant and careless, and their children, of course, so perpetually exposed to everything catching. No, Joe Ralston was certainly right, and Charlotte almost insanely unreasonable. But it would be useless to tell her so now. Instinctively, Delia temporized.

"After all," she whispered to the prone ear, "if it's only after you have children—you may not have any—for some time."

"Oh, yes, I shall!" came back in anguish from the cushions.

Delia smiled with matronly superiority. "Really, Chatty, I don't quite see how you can know. You don't understand."

Charlotte Lovell lifted herself up. Her collar of Brussels lace[80] hung in a crumpled wisp on the loose folds of her bodice, and through the disorder of her hair the white lock glimmered haggardly. In the pale brown of her eyes[81] the little green specks floated like leaves in a trout-pool.

"Poor girl," Delia thought, "how old and ugly she looks! More than ever like an old maid; and she seems to have no idea[82] that she'll never have another chance."

"You must try to be sensible, Chatty dear. After all, one's own babies have the first claim."

"That's just it." The girl seized her fiercely by the wrists. "How can I give up my own baby?"

"Your—your?"[83] Delia's world again began to waver under her. "Which of the poor little waifs, dearest, do you call your own baby?" she questioned patiently.

Charlotte looked her straight in the eyes. "I call my own baby my own baby."

"Your own—? You're hurting my wrists, Chatty."[84] Delia freed herself, forcing a smile. "Your own—?"

"My own little girl: the one that Jessamine and Cyrus—"[85]

"Oh—" Delia Ralston gasped.

The two cousins sat silent, facing each other; but Delia looked away. It came over her with a shudder of repugnance that such things should not have been spoken in her bedroom, so near the spotless nursery across the passage. Mechanically she smoothed the folds of her silk skirt, which her cousin's embrace had crumpled. Then she looked again at Charlotte's eyes, and her own melted.[86]

"Oh, poor Chatty—poor Chatty!"[87] She held out her arms to her cousin.

Chapter II

The shepherd continued to steal his kiss from the shepherdess, and the clock in the fallen trunk continued to tick out the minutes.

Delia, petrified, sat unconscious of their passing, her cousin clasped to her. She was dumb with the horror and amazement of learning that her own blood ran in the veins of the anonymous foundling, the "hundred-dollar baby" about whom New York had so long furtively jested and conjectured. It was her first contact with the nether side of the smooth social surface, and she sickened at the thought that such things were, and that she, Delia Ralston, should be hearing of them in her own house, from the lips of the victim! For Chatty of course was a victim—but whose? She had spoken no name, and Delia could put no question: the horror of it sealed her lips. Her mind had instantly raced back over Chatty's past; but she saw no masculine figure in it but Joe Ralston's. And to connect Joe with the episode was obviously unthinkable. Some one in the South, then? But no: Charlotte had been ill when she left—and in a flash Delia understood the real nature of that illness, and of the girl's disappearance. But from such speculations, too, her mind recoiled, and instinctively she fastened on something she could still grasp: Joe Ralston's attitude about Chatty's paupers. Of course Joe could not let his wife risk bringing home contagion—that was safe ground to dwell on. Her own Jim would have felt in the same way; and she would certainly have agreed with him.[1]

Her eyes traveled back to the clock. She always thought of Clem Spender when she looked at the clock, and suddenly she wondered—if things had been different—what *he* would have said if she had made such an appeal to him as Charlotte had made to Joe. The thing seemed inconceivable; yet in a flash of mental readjustment she saw herself as his wife, she saw her children as his;[2] she pictured herself asking him to let her go on caring for the poor waifs in the Mercer Street stable, and she distinctly heard his laugh and his light answer: "Why on earth did you ask, you little goose? Do you take me for such a Pharisee[3] as that?"

Yes, that was Clem Spender all over—tolerant, reckless, indifferent to consequences, always doing the kind thing at the moment, and too often leaving others to pay the score. "There's something cheap about Clem," Jim had once said in his heavy way. Delia Ralston roused herself and pressed her cousin closer. "Chatty, tell me," she whispered.

"There's nothing more."

"I mean, about yourself—this thing—this—"[4] Clem Spender's voice was still in her ears. "You loved some one," she breathed.

"Yes. That's over.... Now it's only the child.[5].... And I could love Joe—in another way." Chatty Lovell straightened herself, wan and frowning.

"I need the money—I must have it for my baby, or else they'll send it to an institution."[6] She paused. "But that's not all. I want to marry—to be a wife, like all of you. I should have loved Joe's children—our children. Life doesn't stop."

"No: I suppose not. But you speak as if—as if—the person who took advantage of you—"[7]

"No one took advantage of me. I was lonely and unhappy. I met some one who was lonely and unhappy. People don't all have your luck. We were both too poor to marry each other—and Mother would never have consented. And so one day—one day before he said good-by—"[8]

"He said good-by?"

"Yes. He was going to leave the country."

"To leave the country—knowing?"[9]

"How was he to know? He doesn't live here. He'd just come back—come back to see his family—for a few weeks—"[10] She broke off, her thin lips pressed together upon her secret.

———

There was a silence. Delia stared[11] at the bold shepherd.

"Come back from where?" she suddenly asked in a low tone.[12]

"Oh, what does it matter? You wouldn't understand." Charlotte broke off irritably,[13] in the very words her married cousin had compassionately addressed to her virginity.

A slow blush rose to Delia's cheek: she felt oddly humiliated by the rebuke conveyed in that contemptuous retort. She seemed to herself shy, ineffectual, as incapable as an ignorant girl of dealing with the abominations that Charlotte was thrusting on her. But suddenly some fierce feminine intuition struggled and woke in her. She forced her eyes upon her cousin's.

"You wont[14] tell me who it was?"

"What's the use? I haven't told anybody."

"Then why have you come to me?"

Charlotte's stony face broke up in weeping. "It's for my baby— my baby—"[15]

Delia did not heed her. "How can I help you if I don't know?" she insisted in a harsh, dry voice: her heartbeats were so violent that they felt like a throttling hand at her throat.[16]

Charlotte made no answer.

"Come back from where?" Delia doggedly repeated; and at that, with a long wail, the girl flung her hands up, screening her eyes. "He always thought you'd wait for him," she sobbed out, "and then, when he found you hadn't—and that you were marrying Jim— He heard it just as he was sailing. . . . . He didn't know it till Mrs. Mingott asked him to bring the clock for your wedding—"[17]

"Stop—stop," Delia cried, springing to her feet. She had provoked the avowal, and now that it had come, she felt that it had been gratuitously and indecently thrust upon her. Was this New York, *her* New York, her safe, friendly, hypocritical New York, was this James Ralston's house, and this his wife listening to such revelations of dishonor?[18]

—

Charlotte stood up in her turn. "I knew it—I knew it! You think worse of my baby now, instead of better. . . . Oh, why did you make me tell you? I knew you'd never understand. I'd always cared for him, ever since I came out; that was why I wouldn't marry anyone else. But I knew there was no hope for me—he never looked at anybody but you. And then, when he came back four years ago, and there was no *you* for him any more, he began to notice me, to be kind, to talk to me about his life and his painting—" She drew a deep breath, and her voice cleared. "That's over—all over. It's as if I couldn't either hate him or love him. There's only the child now—my child. He doesn't even know of it—why should he? It's none of his business; it's nobody's business but mine. But surely you must see I can't give up my baby."[19]

Delia Ralston stood speechless, looking away from her cousin in a grow-in horror.[20] She had lost all sense of reality, all feeling of safety and self-reliance. Her impulse was to close her ears to the other's appeal as a child buries its head from midnight terrors. At last she drew herself up, and spoke with dry lips.

"But what do you mean to do? Why have you come to me? Why have you told me all this?"

"Because he loved you!" Charlotte Lovell stammered out; and the two women stood and faced each other.

Slowly the tears rose to Delia's eyes and rolled down her cheeks, moistening her lips. Through them she saw her cousin's haggard countenance waver and droop like a drowning face under water. Things half guessed, obscurely felt, surged up from unsuspected depths in her. It was almost as if, for a moment, this other woman were telling her of her own secret past, putting into crude words all the trembling silences of her heart.[21]

The worst of it was, as Charlotte said, that they must act now; there was not a day to lose. Chatty was right—it was impossible that she should marry Joe if to do so meant giving up the child. But in any case, how could she marry him without telling him the truth? And was it conceivable that, after hearing it, he should not repudiate her? All these questions spun agonizingly through Delia's brain, and through them glimmered the persistent vision of the child—Clem Spender's child—growing up on charity, in a negro hovel, or herded in one of the plague-houses they called asylums.[22] No: the child came first—she felt it in every fiber of her body. But what should she do, of whom take counsel, how advise the wretched creature who had come to her in Clement's name? Delia glanced about her desperately, and then turned back to her cousin.[23]

"You must give me time. I must think. You ought not to marry him—and yet all the arrangements are made; and the wedding presents. . . . . There would be a scandal. . . . . It would kill Granny Lovell."[24]

Charlotte answered in a low voice: "There *is* no time. I must decide now."

Delia pressed her hands against her breast. "I tell you I must think. I wish you would go home—or, no: stay here—your mother mustn't see your eyes. Jim's not coming home till late; you can wait in this room till I come back." She had opened the wardrobe, and was reaching up for a plain bonnet and heavy veil.[25]

"Stay here? But where are you going?"

"I don't know. I want to walk—to get the air. I think I want to be alone." Feverishly she had unfolded[26] her Paisley shawl, tied on bonnet and veil, thrust her mittened hands into her muff.[27] Charlotte, without moving, stared at her dumbly from the sofa.

"You'll wait?" Delia insisted,[28] on the threshold.

"Yes; I'll wait."[29]

Delia shut the door and hurried down the stairs.

CHAPTER III

She had spoken the truth in saying that she did not know where she was going. She simply wanted to get away from Charlotte's unbearable face, and from the immediate atmosphere of her tragedy. Outside, in the open, perhaps it would be easier to think.

As she skirted the park-rails, she saw her rosy children playing, under their nurse's eye, with the pampered progeny of other Park-dwellers. The little girl had on her new plaid velvet bonnet and white tippet, and the boy his Highland cap and broadcloth spencer.[1] How happy and jolly they looked! The nurse spied her, but she shook her head, waved at the group and hurried on.

She walked and walked through the familiar streets decked with bright winter sunshine. It was early afternoon, an hour when the gentlemen had just returned to their offices, and there were few pedestrians in Irving Place and Union Square. Delia crossed the Square to Broadway.

The Lovell house in Mercer Street was a sturdy, old-fashioned brick dwelling. A large stable adjoined it, opening on an alley such as Delia, on her honeymoon trip to England, had heard called a "mews."[2] She turned into the alley, entered the stable court, and pushed open a door. In a shabby whitewashed room a dozen children, gathered about a stove, were playing with broken toys. The Irishwoman who had charge of them was cutting out small garments on a broken-legged deal table.[3] She raised a friendly face, recognizing Delia as the lady who had once or twice been to see the children with Miss Charlotte.[4]

———

Delia paused, embarrassed.

"I—I came to ask if you need any new toys," she stammered.

"That we do, ma'am. And many another thing too, though Miss Charlotte tells me I'm not to beg of the ladies that comes to see our poor darlin's."

"Oh, you may beg of me, Bridget," Mrs. Ralston answered, smiling. "Let me see your babies—it's so long since I've been here."

The children had stopped playing, and huddled against their nurse, gazed up open-mouthed at the rich, rustling lady. One little girl with pale brown eyes and scarlet cheeks was dressed in a plaid alpaca[5] frock trimmed with imitation coral buttons that Delia remembered. They had been on Charlotte's "best-dress" the year she came out. Delia stooped and took up the child. Its curly hair was brown, the exact color of the eyes—thank heaven! But the eyes had the same little green spangles floating in their transparency. Delia sat down, and the little girl, standing on her knee, gravely fingered her watch-chain.[6]

"Oh, ma'am—maybe her shoes'll soil your skirt. The floor aint none too clean."[7]

Delia shook her head, and pressed the child against her. She had forgotten the other gazing babies and their wardress. The little creature on her knee was made of different stuff[8]—it had not needed the plaid alpaca and coral buttons to single her out. Her brown curls grew in points on her high forehead, exactly as Clement Spender's did. Delia laid a burning cheek against the forehead.

"Baby want my lovely yellow chain?"

Baby did.

Delia unfastened it and hung it about the child's neck. The other babies clapped and crowed, but the little girl, gravely dimpling, continued to finger the chain in silence.[9]

"Oh, ma'am, you can't leave that fine chain on little Teeny. When she has to go back to those blacks—"[10]

"What is her name?"

"Teena they call her, I believe. It don't seem a Christian name, har'ly."

Delia was silent.

"What I say is, her cheeks is too red. And she coughs too easy. Always one cold and another. Here, Teeny, leave the lady go."

Delia stood up, loosening the tender arms.

"She doesn't want to leave go of you, ma'am. Miss Chatty ain't been in yet, and she's kinder lonesome without her. She don't play like the other children, somehow..... Teeny, you look at that lovely chain you've got..... There, there now!"[11]

"Good-by, Clementina," Delia whispered below her breath. She kissed the pale brown eyes, the curly crown, and dropped her veil on rushing tears. In the stableyard[12] she dried them on her large embroidered handkerchief, and stood hesitating. Then with a decided step she turned toward home.

The house was as she had left it, except that the children had come in; she heard them romping in the nursery as she went down the passage to her bedroom. Charlotte Lovell was seated on the sofa, upright and rigid, as Delia had left her.

"Chatty—Chatty, I've thought it out. Listen: Whatever happens, the baby sha'n't stay with those people. I mean to keep her."[13]

Charlotte stood up, tall and white. The eyes in her thin face had grown so dark that they seemed like spectral hollows in a skull. She opened her lips to speak; and then, snatching at her handkerchief, pressed it to her mouth and sank down again. A red trickle dripped through the handkerchief onto her poplin skirt.[14]

"Charlotte—Charlotte!"[15] Delia screamed, on her knees beside her cousin. Charlotte's head slid back against the cushions, and the trickle ceased. She closed her eyes, and Delia, seizing a vinaigrette from the dressing-table, held it to her pinched nostrils. The room was filled with an acrid aromatic scent.[16]

Charlotte's lids lifted. "Don't be frightened. I still spit blood sometimes—not often. My lung is nearly healed. But it's the terror—"

"No, no: there's to be no more terror. I tell you I've thought it all out. Jim is going to let me take the baby."

The girl raised herself haggardly. "Jim? Have you told him? Is that where you've been?"

"No, darling. I've only been to see the baby."

"Oh!" Charlotte moaned,[17] leaning back again. Delia took her own handkerchief, and wiped away the tears that were raining down her cousin's cheeks.

"You mustn't cry, Chatty; you must be brave. Your little girl and his—how could you think? But you must give me time: I must manage it in my own way. . . . . Only trust me."[18]

Charlotte's lips stirred faintly.

"The tears—don't dry them, Delia. I like to feel them."[19]

———

The two cousins leaned against each other without speaking. The ormolu clock ticked out the measure of their mute communion in minutes, quarters, a half-hour, then an hour: the day declined and darkened; the shadows lengthened across the garlands of the Axminster carpet and the broad white bed. There was a knock.[20]

"The children's waiting to say their grace before supper, ma'am."

"Yes, Eliza. Let them say it to you. I'll come later." As the nurse's steps receded, Charlotte Lovell disengaged herself from Delia's embrace.

"Now I can go," she said.

"You're not too weak, dear? I can send for a coach to take you home."

"No, no; it would frighten Mother.[21] And I shall like walking now, in the darkness. Sometimes the world used to seem all one awful glare to me. There were days when I thought the sun would never set. And then there was the moon at night." She laid her hands on her cousin's shoulders. "Now it's different. By and by I sha'n't hate the light."

The two women kissed each other, and Delia whispered: "To-morrow."

Chapter IV

The Ralstons gave up old customs reluctantly; but once they had adopted a new one, they found it impossible to understand why everyone else did not do likewise.[1]

When Delia, who came of the laxer Lovells, and was naturally inclined to novelty, had first proposed to her husband to dine at six o'clock instead of two, his malleable young face had become as relentless as that of the old original Ralston in his grim Colonial portrait. But after a two days' resistance,[2] he had come round to his wife's view, and now smiled contemptuously at the obstinacy of those who clung to a heavy midday meal and high tea.

"There's nothing I hate like narrow-mindedness. Let people eat when they like, for all I care: it's their narrow-mindedness that I can't stand."

Delia was thinking of this as she sat in the drawing-room (her mother would have called it the parlor) waiting for her husband's return. She had just had time to smooth her glossy braids, and slip on the black-and-white striped silk with cherry pipings which was his favorite dress. The drawing-room, with its Nottingham lace curtains[3] looped back under florid gilt cornices, its marble center-table on a carved rosewood foot, and its old-fashioned mahogany armchairs covered with one of the new French silk damasks, in a tart shade of apple-green, was one for any young wife to be proud of. The rosewood whatnots[4] on each side of the folding doors that led into the dining-room were adorned with tropical shells, feldspar vases, an alabaster model of the Leaning Tower of Pisa, a pair of obelisks made of scraps of porphyry and serpentine picked up by the young couple in the Roman Forum, a small bust of Clytie in *biscuit de Sèvres,* and four old-fashioned figures of the Seasons in Chelsea ware, that had to be left among the newer knick-knacks[5] because they had belonged to Great-grandmamma Ralston. On the damask wall-paper hung large dark steel-engravings of Cole's "Voyage of Life," and on the table lay handsomely tooled copies of Turner's "Rivers of France," Drake's "Culprit Fay," Crabbe's "Tales," and "The Book of Beauty," containing portraits of the British peeresses who had participated in the Earl of Eglinton's tournament.[6]

As Delia sat there, before the hard-coal fire[7] in its arched opening of black marble, her citron-wood[8] work-table at her side, and one of the new French lamps shedding a pleasant light on the center-table from under a crystal-fringed shade, she asked herself how she could have passed, in such a short time, so completely out of her usual circle of impressions and convictions—so much farther than ever before beyond the Ralston horizon. Here it was, closing in on her again, as if the very plaster ornaments of the ceiling, the forms of the furniture, the cut of her dress, had been built out of Ralston prejudices, and turned to adamant by the touch of Ralston hands.

She must have been mad, she thought, to have committed herself so far to Charlotte; yet turn about as she would[9] in the ever-tightening circle of the problem, she could still discover[10] no other issue. Somehow, it lay with her to save Clem Spender's baby.

She heard the sound of the latchkey (her heart had never beat so high at it), and the putting down of a tall hat on the hall console—or two tall hats, was it? The drawing-room door opened, and two high-stocked and ample-coated young men came in—two Jim Ralstons, so to speak. Delia had never before noticed how much her husband and his cousin Joe were alike: it made her feel how justified she was in always thinking of the Ralstons collectively.[11]

She would not have been young, and tender, and a happy wife, if she had not thought Joe but an indifferent copy of her Jim; yet allowing for defects in the reproduction, there remained a striking likeness between the two tall, athletic figures, the short, sanguine faces with straight noses, straight whiskers, straight brows, the candid blue eyes and sweet, selfish smiles. Only, at the present moment, Joe looked like Jim with a toothache.[12]

"Look here, my dear: here's a young man who's asked to take potluck[13] with us." Jim smiled, with the confidence of a well-nourished husband who knows that he can always bring a friend home unannounced.[14]

"How nice of you, Joe! —Do you suppose he can put up with oyster soup and a stuffed goose?" Delia beamed upon her husband.

"I knew it! I told you so, my dear chap! He said you wouldn't like it—that you'd be fussed about the dinner. Wait till you're married, Joseph Ralston!"[15] Jim brought down a genial paw on his cousin's bottle-green shoulder, and Joe grimaced as if the tooth had stabbed him.

"It's excessively kind of you, Cousin Delia, to take me in this evening. The fact is—"

"Dinner first, my boy, if you don't mind! A bottle of Burgundy will brush away the blue devils. Your arm to your cousin, please; I'll just go and see that the wine is brought up."

—

Oyster soup, broiled shad, stuffed goose, corn fritters[16] and green peppers, followed by one of Grand-mamma Ralston's famous caramel custards: through all her mental anguish, Delia was faintly aware of a secret pride in her achievement. Certainly it would serve to confirm the rumor[17] that Jim Ralston could always bring a friend home to dine without notice. The Ralston and Lovell wines rounded off the effect, and even Joe's drawn face had mellowed by the time the Lovell Madeira[18] started westward. Delia marked the change when the two young men rejoined her in the drawing-room.

"And now, my dear fellow, you'd better tell her the whole story," Jim counseled,[19] pushing an armchair toward his cousin.

The young woman, bent above her wool-work,[20] listened with lowered lids and flushed cheeks. As a married woman—as a mother—Joe hoped she would think him justified in speaking to her frankly: he had her husband's authority to do so.

"Oh, go ahead, go ahead," chafed the exuberant after-dinner Jim from the hearth-rug.

Delia listened, considered, let the bridegroom flounder on through his exposition. Her needle hung like a sword of Damocles[21] above the canvas: she saw at once that Joe depended on her trying to win Charlotte over to his way of thinking. But he was very much in love; at a word from Delia, she understood that he would yield, and Charlotte gain her point, save the child, and marry him.[22]

How easy it was, after all! A friendly welcome, a good dinner, a ripe wine, and[23] the memory of Charlotte's eyes—so much the more expressive for all that they had looked upon. A secret envy stabbed the wife who had lacked this last enlightenment.

How easy it was—and yet it must not be! Whatever happened, she could not let Charlotte Lovell marry Joe Ralston. All the traditions of honor and probity in which she had been brought up forbade her to connive at such a plan. She could conceive—had already conceived—of high-handed measures, swift and adroit defiances of precedent, subtle revolts against the heartlessness of social routine. But a lie she could never connive at. The idea of Charlotte's marrying Joe Ralston—her own Jim's cousin—without revealing her past to him seemed to Delia as dishonorable as it would have seemed to any Ralston. And to tell him the truth would at once put an end to the marriage; of that even Chatty was aware. Social tolerance was not dealt in the same measure to men and to women, and neither Delia nor Charlotte had ever wondered why: like all the young women of their class, they simply bowed to the ineluctable.[23]

No: there was no escape from the dilemma. As clearly as it was Delia's duty to save Clem Spender's child, so clearly, also, she seemed destined to sacrifice his mistress. As the thought pressed on her, she remembered Charlotte's wistful cry, "I want to be married, like all of you," and her heart tightened. But yet it must not be.[24]

———

"I make every allowance," Joe was droning on, "for my sweet girl's ignorance and inexperience—for her lovely purity. How could a man wish his future wife to be—to be otherwise? You're with me, Jim? And Delia? I've told her, you understand, that she shall always have a special sum for her poor children, in addition to her pin-money—on that she may absolutely count. God! I'm willing to draw up a deed, a settlement, before a lawyer, if she says so. I admire. I appreciate her generosity. But I ask you, Delia, as a mother—mind you, now, I want your frank opinion. If you think I can stretch a point—can let her go on giving her personal care to the children until—until,"—a flush of pride suffused the potential father's brow,—"till nearer duties claim her. . . . . Why, I'm more than ready—if you'll tell her so, I undertake." Joe proclaimed, suddenly tingling with the memory of his last glass, "to make it right with my mother, whose prejudices, of course, while I respect them, I can never allow to—to come between me and my own convictions." He sprang to his feet, and beamed on his dauntless double in the chimney-mirror. "My convictions," he flung back at it.[25]

"Hear, hear!" cried Jim emotionally.

Delia's needle gave the canvas a sharp prick, and she pushed her work aside.

"I think I understand you both, Joe. Certainly, in Charlotte's place, I should never give up those children."[26]

"There you are, my dear fellow!" Jim triumphed, as proud of this vicarious courage as of the perfection of the dinner.

"Never," said Delia. "Especially, I mean, the foundlings—there are two, I think. Those children always die if they are sent to asylums. That is what is haunting Chatty."

"Poor innocents! How I love her for loving them! That there should be such scoundrels upon this earth unpunished![27] Delia, will you tell her that I'll do whatever—"

"Gently, old man, gently," Jim admonished,[28] with a flash of Ralston caution.

"Well, whatever—in reason—"[29]

Delia lifted an arresting hand. "I'll tell her, Joe: she will be grateful. But it's of no use."

"No use? What more—"[30]

"Nothing more—except this.[31] Charlotte has had a return of her old illness. She coughed blood here today. You must not marry her."

There: it was done. She stood up, trembling in every bone, and feeling herself pale to the lips. Had she done right? Had she done wrong? And would she ever know?

Poor Joe turned on her a face as wan as hers: he clutched the back of his armchair, his head drooping forward like an old man's. His lips moved, but made no sound.

"My God!" Jim stammered. "But you know you've got to pull yourself together, old boy."[32]

"I'm—I'm so sorry for you, Joe. She'll tell you tomorrow."[33] Delia faltered, while her husband continued to proffer heavy consolations.

"Take it like a man, old chap. Think of yourself—your future. Can't be, you know. Delia's right[34]—she always *is*. Better get it over—better face the music now than later."

"Now than later," Joe echoed with a tortured grin; and it occurred to Delia that never before in the course of his easy, good-natured[35] life had he had—any more than her Jim—to give up anything his heart was set on. Even the vocabulary of renunciation, and its conventional gestures, were unfamiliar to him.

"But I don't understand. I can't give her up," he declared, blinking away boyish tears.[36]

"Think of the children, my dear fellow; it's your duty," Jim admonished him,[37] checking a glance of pride at Delia's wholesome comeliness.

In the long conversation that followed between the cousins—argument, counter-argument, sage counsel and hopeless protest—Delia took but an occasional part. She knew well enough what the end would be. The bridegroom who had feared that his bride might bring home contagion from her visits to the poor would not knowingly implant disease in his race. Nor was that all. Too many sad instances of mothers prematurely fading, and leaving their husbands alone with a young flock to rear, must be pressing upon Joe's memory. Ralstons, Lovells, Lannings, Archers, Van der Luydens—which one of them had not some grave to care for in a distant cemetery, graves of young relatives "in a decline," sent abroad to be cured by balmy Italy?[38] The Protestant graveyards of Rome and Pisa were full of New York names; and the vision of that familiar pilgrimage with a dying wife was one to turn the most ardent Ralston cold. And all the while, as she listened with bent head, Delia kept repeating to herself: "This is easy; but how am I to tell Charlotte?"[39]

When poor Joe, late that evening, wrung her hand with a stammered farewell, she called him back abruptly.[40]

"You must let me see her first, please; you must wait till she sends for you." And she winced a little at the alacrity of his acceptance. But no amount of rhetorical bolstering-up could make it easy for a young man to face what lay ahead of Joe; and her final glance at him was one of compassion.[41]

———

The front door closed upon Joe, and she was roused by her husband's touch on her shoulder.

"I never admired you more, darling. My wise Delia!"

Her head bent back, she took his kiss; and then drew away.[42] The sparkle in his eyes she understood to be as much an invitation to her bloom as a tribute to her sagacity.

"What should you have done, Jim,[43] if I'd had to tell you about myself what I've just told Joe about Chatty?"

A slight frown showed that he thought the question negligible, and hardly in her usual taste. "Come!" His strong arm entreated her.[44]

She continued to stand away from him, with grave eyes. "Poor Chatty! Nothing left now—"

His own eyes grew grave in sympathy.[45] At such moments he was still the sentimental boy whom she could manage.

"Ah, poor Chatty, indeed!" He groped for the readiest panacea.

"Lucky, after all, she has those paupers, isn't it? I suppose a woman *must* have children to love—somebody else's, if not her own." It was evident that the remedy had already relieved his pain.[46]

"Yes," she agreed, "I see no other comfort for her. I'm sure Joe will feel that too. Between us, darling,"—and now she let him have her hands,[47]—"between us, you and I must see to it that she keeps her babies."

"Her babies?" He smiled at the possessive pronoun. "Of course, poor girl! Unless she's sent to Italy?"[48]

"Oh, she wont be that—where's the money to come from? And besides, she'd never leave Aunt Lovell. But I thought, dear, if I might tell her tomorrow,—you see, I'm not exactly looking forward to my talk with her,—if I might tell her that you would let me look after the baby she's most worried about, the poor little foundling girl who has no name and no home,—if I might put aside a fixed sum from my pin-money—"[49]

Their hands glowed together;[50] she lifted her flushing face to his. Manly tears were in his eyes: ah, how he triumphed in her health, her wisdom, her generosity!

"Not a penny from your pin-money!"[51]

She feigned discouragement and wonder. "Think, dear—if I'd had to give you up!"

"Not a penny from your pin-money, I say—but as much more as you need, to help poor Chatty's pauper. There—will that content you?"

"Dearest! When I think of our own upstairs!"[52] They held each other, awed by that evocation.

CHAPTER V

Charlotte Lovell, at the sound of her cousin's step on the thresh-old,[1] lifted a fevered face from the pillow. The bedroom, dim and close, smelt of eau de Cologne and fresh linen. Delia, blinking in from the bright winter sun, had to feel her way through a twilight obstructed by dark mahogany.

"I want to see your face, Chatty—unless[2] your head aches too much?"

Charlotte sighed, "No," and Delia drew back the heavy window-curtains and let a ray of light into the room. In it, she saw the girl's head livid against the bed-linen, the brick-red circles again visible under darkly shadowed lids. Just so poor Cousin So-and-so had looked, the week before she sailed for Italy![3]

"Delia!" Charlotte breathed.

Delia approached[4] the bed, and stood looking down at her cousin with new eyes. Yes: it had been easy enough, the night be-fore, to dispose of Chatty's future as if it were her own—but now?[5]

"Darling—"

"Oh, begin, please," the girl interrupted, "or I shall know that what's coming is too dreadful!"

"Chatty, dearest, if I promised you too much—"

"Jim wont let you take my child? I knew it! Shall I always go on dreaming things that can never be?"

Delia, her tears running down, knelt by the bed and gave her fresh hand into the other's burning clutch.

"Don't think that, dear; think only of what you'd like best."[6]

"Like best?" The girl rose sharply[7] against her pillows, alive to the hot fingertips.

"You can't marry Joe, dear—can you—and keep little Tina?" Delia continued.

"Not keep her with me, no—but somewhere where I could slip off to see her. Oh, I had hoped such follies!"[8]

"Give up follies, Charlotte. Keep her where? See your own child in secret? Always in dread of disgrace? Of wrong to your other children? Have you ever thought of that?"

"Oh, my poor head wont think! You're trying to tell me that I must give her up?"

"No, dear—but that you must not marry Joe."[9]

Charlotte sank back on the pillow, her eyes half-closed. "I tell you I must make my child a home. Delia, you're too blessed to understand!"

"Think yourself blessed too, Chatty. You sha'n't give up your baby. She shall live with you: you shall take care of her—for me."

"For you?"

"I promised you I'd take her, didn't I? But not that you should marry Joe. Only that I would make a home for your baby. Well, that's done: you shall always be together."[10]

Charlotte clung to her and sobbed. "But Joe—I can't tell him, I can't." She put back Delia suddenly. "You haven't told him of my—of my baby? I couldn't bear to hurt him as much as that."

"I told him that you coughed blood yesterday. He'll see you presently: he's dreadfully unhappy. He considers that,[11] in view of your bad health, the engagement is broken by your wish—and he accepts your decision; but if he weakens, or if you weaken, I can do nothing for you or for little Tina. For heaven's sake, remember that."

Delia released her hold, and Charlotte leaned back silent, with closed eyes. On a chair near the bed lay the poplin with red velvet ribbons which had been made over in honor of her betrothal. A pair of new slippers of bronze kid[12] peeped from beneath its folds. Poor Chatty! She had hardly had time to be pretty.

Delia sat by the bed motionless, her eyes on the closed face. They followed the course of two tears that forced a way between Charlotte's tight lids, hung on the lashes, glittered slowly down the cheeks. As the tears reached Chatty's lips, she spoke.[13]

"Shall I live with her somewhere, do you mean? Just she and I?"[14]

"Just you and she."

"In a little house?"

"In a little house."[15]

"You're sure, Delia?"

"Sure, my dearest."

Charlotte once more raised herself on her elbow and slipped a hand under her pillow. She drew out a narrow ribbon on which hung a diamond cluster ring.[16]

"I had taken it off already," she said,[17] and handed it to Delia.

Chapter VI

Everyone agreed afterward that you could always have told that Charlotte Lovell was meant to be an old maid. Even before her illness, it had been manifest: there was something prim about her, in spite of her fiery hair. Lucky enough for her, poor girl, considering her wretched health in her youth: Mrs. James Ralston's contemporaries, for instance, remembered Charlotte as a mere ghost, coughing her lungs out—that, of course, had been the reason for breaking her engagement with Joe Ralston.[1]

True, she had recovered very rapidly, in spite of the peculiar treatment she was given. The Lovells, as everyone knew, couldn't afford to send her to Italy; so she was packed off to a farmhouse on the Hudson,—a little place on the James Ralstons' property,—where she lived for five or six years with an Irish servant-woman and a foundling baby. The story of the foundling was another queer episode in Charlotte's history. From the time of her first illness, when she was only twenty-two or -three, she had developed an almost morbid tenderness for children, especially for the children of the poor. It was said—Dr. Lanskell was understood to have said—that the baffled instinct of motherhood was peculiarly intense in cases where lung-disease prevented marriage. And so, when the

Doctor decided that Chatty must break her engagement to Jim Ralston and go to live in the country, the Doctor had told her family that the only hope of saving her lay in not separating her entirely from her poor children, but in letting her choose one of them, the youngest and most pitiable, and devote herself to its care. So the James Ralstons had lent her their little farmhouse; and Mrs. Jim, with her extraordinary gift of taking things in at a glance, had at once arranged everything, and even pledged herself to look after the baby if Charlotte died.[2]

Charlotte did not die till long afterward. She lived to grow robust and middle-aged, energetic and even tyrannical. And as the transformation in her character took place, she became more and more like the typical old maid: precise, methodical, absorbed in trifles, and attaching an exaggerated importance to the smallest social and domestic observances. Such was her reputation as a vigilant housewife that when poor Jim Ralston was killed by a fall from his horse, and left Delia, still young, with a boy and girl to bring up, it seemed perfectly natural that the heartbroken widow should take her cousin to live with her and share her task.[3]

But Delia Ralston never did things quite like other people. When she took Charlotte, she took Charlotte's foundling too—a little dark-haired girl with pale brown eyes, and the odd, incisive manner of children who have lived too much alone. The little girl was called Tina Lovell: it was vaguely supposed that Charlotte had adopted her. She grew up on terms of affectionate equality with her young Ralston cousins, and almost as much so—it might be said— with the two women who mothered her. But by a natural instinct of imitation which no one thought it necessary to correct, she always called Delia Ralston "Mamma," and Charlotte Lovell "Aunt Chatty." She was a brilliant and engaging creature, and people marveled at poor Chatty's luck in having chosen so interesting a specimen among her foundlings—for she was by this time supposed to have had a whole asylumful to choose from.[4]

The agreeable elderly bachelor, Sillerton Jackson, returning from a prolonged sojourn in Paris (where he was understood to have been made much of by the highest personages), pronounced himself immensely struck with Tina's charms when he saw her at her coming-out ball, and asked Delia's permission to come some evening and dine alone with her and her young people. He complimented the widow on the rosy beauty of her own young Delia; but the mother's keen eye perceived that all the while he was watching Tina, and after dinner he confided to the older ladies that there was something "very French" in the girl's way of doing her hair, and that in the capital of all the elegances she would have been pronounced extremely stylish.[5]

"Oh—" Delia deprecated beamingly,[6] while Charlotte Lovell sat bent over her work with pinched lips; but Tina, who had been laughing with her cousins at the other end of the room, was around upon her elders in a flash.

"I heard what Mr. Sillerton said! Yes, I did, Mamma: he says I do my hair stylishly. Didn't I always tell you so? I *know* it's more becoming to let it curl as it wants to than to plaster it down with bandoline[7] like Aunty's—"

"Tina, Tina—you always think people are admiring you!" Miss Lovell protested.

"Why shouldn't I, when they do?" the girl laughingly challenged; and turning her mocking eyes[8] on Sillerton Jackson: "Do tell Aunt Charlotte not to be so dreadfully old-maidish!"

Delia saw the blood rise to Charlotte Lovell's face. It no longer painted two brick-rose circles on her thin cheek-bones, but diffused a harsh flush over her whole countenance, from the collar fastened with an old-fashioned garnet brooch to the pepper-and-salt hair (with no trace of red left in it) flattened down over her hollow temples.

That evening, when they went up to bed, Delia called Tina into her room.

"You ought not to speak to your Aunt Charlotte as you did just now, dear. It's disrespectful—and it hurts her."[9]

The girl overflowed with compunction. "Oh, I'm so sorry! Because I said she was an old maid? But she *is*, isn't she, Mamma? In her inmost soul, I mean. I don't believe she's ever been young—

ever thought of fun or admiration or falling in love—do you? That's why she never understands me, and you always do, you darling dear Mamma." With one of her light movements Tina was in the widow's arms.

"Child, child!" Delia softly scolded, kissing the dark curls planted in five points on the girl's forehead.[10]

—

There was a footfall in the passage, and Charlotte Lovell stood in the doorway. Delia, without moving, gave her a glance of welcome over Tina's shoulder.[11]

"Come in, Charlotte. I'm scolding this child[12] for behaving like a spoilt baby before Sillerton Jackson. What will he think of her?"

"Just what she deserves, probably," Charlotte returned with a cold smile. Tina went toward her, and she kissed the girl's proffered forehead just where Delia's warm lips had touched it. "Good night, child," she said, in her dry tone of dismissal.[13]

The door closed on the two women, and Delia signed to Charlotte to take the armchair opposite her own.

"Not so near the fire," Miss Lovell answered. She chose a straight-backed chair, and sat down with folded hands. Delia's eyes rested absently on the thin, ringless hands: she wondered why Charlotte never wore her mother's jewels.[14]

"I heard[15] what you were saying to Tina, Delia. You were scolding her because she called me an old maid."

It was Delia's turn to color. "I scolded her for being disrespectful, dear; if you heard what I said, you can't think that I was too severe."

"Not too severe: no. I've never thought you too severe with Tina: on the contrary."[16]

"You think I spoil her?"

"Sometimes."

Delia felt an unreasoning resentment. "What was it I said that you object to?"

Charlotte returned her glance steadily. "I would rather she thought me an old maid than—"

"Oh—" Delia murmured. With one of her quick leaps of intuition, she had entered into the other's soul, and measured its shuddering loneliness.[17]

"What else," Charlotte inexorably pursued, "*can* she possibly be allowed to think me—ever?"

"I see—I see—"[18] the widow faltered.

"A ridiculous, narrow-minded old maid[19]—nothing else," Charlotte Lovell insisted, getting to her feet, "or I shall never feel safe with her."

"Good night, my dear," Delia said compassionately. There were moments when she almost hated Charlotte for being Tina's mother, and others, such as this, when her heart was wrung by the tragic spectacle of that unavowed bond.

Charlotte seemed to have divined her thought.

"Oh, but don't pity me! She's mine," she murmured, going.

CHAPTER VII

Delia Ralston sometimes felt that the real events of her life did not begin until both her children had contracted—ever so safely and suitably—the usual irreproachable New York alliances.[1] The boy had married first, choosing a Vandergrave in whose father's bank at Albany he was to have an immediate junior partnership; and young Delia (as her mother had foreseen she would) had selected John Junius, the safest and soundest of the many young Halseys, and followed him to his parents' house the year after her brother's marriage.

After young Delia left the house in Gramercy Park, it was inevitable that Tina should take the center front of its narrow stage. Tina had reached the marriageable age; she was admired and sought after; but what hope was there of her finding a husband? The two watchful women did not propound this question to each other; but Delia Ralston, brooding over it day by day, and taking it up with her when she mounted at night to her old-fashioned bedroom, knew that Charlotte Lovell, at the same hour, carried the same problem with her to the floor above.[2]

The two cousins, during their eight years of life together, had seldom openly disagreed. Indeed, it might almost have been said that there was nothing open in their relation. Delia would have had it otherwise: after they had once looked so deeply into each other's souls,[3] it seemed unnatural that a veil should fall between them. But she understood that Tina's ignorance of her origin must at all costs be preserved, and that Charlotte Lovell, abrupt, passionate and inarticulate, knew of no other security than to wall herself up in perpetual silence.

So far had she carried this self-imposed reticence that Mrs. Ralston was surprised at her suddenly asking, soon after young Delia's marriage, to be allowed to move down into the small bedroom next to Tina's, left vacant by the bride's departure.[4]

"But you'll be so much less comfortable there, Chatty. Have you thought of that? Or is it on account of the stairs?"

"No; it's not the stairs," Charlotte answered with her usual bluntness. How could she avail herself of the pretext Delia offered her, when Delia knew that she still ran up and down the three flights like a girl? "It's because I should be next to Tina," she said, in a low voice that jarred like an untuned string.

"Oh—very well. As you please." Mrs. Ralston could not tell why she felt suddenly irritated by the request, unless it were that she had already amused herself with the idea of fitting up the vacant room as a sitting-room for Tina. She had meant to do it in pink and pale green, like an opening flower.

"Of course, if there is any reason—" Charlotte suggested, as if reading her thought.

"None whatever, except that—well, I'd meant to surprise Tina by doing the room up as a sort of little boudoir, where she could have her books and things, and see her girl friends."[5]

"You're too kind, Delia; but Tina mustn't have boudoirs." Miss Lovell answered ironically, the green specks showing in her eyes.

"Very well: as you please," Delia repeated in the same irritated tone. "I'll have your things brought down tomorrow."

Charlotte paused in the doorway. "You're sure there's no other reason?"

"Other reason? Why should there be?" The two women looked at each other almost with hostility, and Charlotte turned to go.

The talk once over, Delia was annoyed with herself for having yielded to Charlotte's wish. Why must it always be she who gave in, she who, after all, was the mistress of the house, and to whom both Charlotte and Tina might almost be said to owe their very existence, or at least all that made it worth having? Yet whenever any question arose about the girl, it was invariably Charlotte who gained her point, Delia who yielded: it was as if Charlotte, in her mute, obstinate way, were determined to take every advantage of the dependence that made it impossible for a woman of Delia's nature to oppose her.[6]

In truth, Delia had looked forward more than she knew to the quiet talks with Tina to which the little boudoir would have lent itself. While her own daughter inhabited the room, Mrs. Ralston had been in the habit of spending an hour there every evening, chatting with the two girls while they undressed, and listening to their comments on the incidents of the day. She always knew beforehand exactly what her own girl would say; but Tina's views and opinions were a perpetual delicious shock to her. Not that they were unfamiliar: there were moments when they seemed to well straight up from the dumb depths of her own past. Only they expressed feelings that she had never uttered, ideas she had hardly avowed to herself: Tina sometimes said things which Delia Ralston, in far-off self-communions, had imagined herself saying to Clem Spender.[7]

And now there would be an end to these evening talks: if Charlotte had asked to be lodged next to her daughter, might it not conceivably be because she wished them to end? It had never before occurred to Delia that her influence over Tina might be resented; now it flashed a light far down into the abyss which had always divided the two women. But a moment later Delia reproached herself for attributing feelings of jealousy to her cousin. Was it not rather to herself that she should have ascribed them? Charlotte, as Tina's mother, had every right to wish to be near her, near her in all senses of the word: what claim had Delia to oppose to that natural privilege? Next morning she ordered Charlotte's things taken down to the room next to Tina's.[8]

That evening, when bedtime came, Charlotte and Tina went upstairs together; but Delia lingered in the drawing-room on the pretext of having letters to write. In truth, she dreaded to pass the threshold where, evening after evening, the fresh laughter of the two girls had waylaid her, while Charlotte Lovell already slept her old-maid sleep on the floor above. It sent a pang through Delia to think that henceforth she would be cut off from this means of keeping her hold on Tina.[9]

An hour later, when she mounted the stairs in her turn, she was guiltily conscious of moving as noiselessly as she could along the heavy carpet of the corridor, and of pausing longer than was necessary over the extinguishing of the gas-jet[10] on the landing. As she stood there she strained her ears for the sound of voices from the doors behind which Charlotte and Tina slept; she would have been secretly hurt at hearing talk and laughter from within. But none came to her; nor was there any light beneath the doors. Evidently Charlotte, in her hard, methodical way, had said good night to her daughter on reaching her room, and gone straight to bed as usual. Perhaps she had never approved of Tina's vigils, of the long undressing punctuated with mirth and confidences; it was not unlikely, Delia reflected, that she had asked to have the room next to her daughter's simply because she wished the girl not to miss her "beauty sleep."[11]

Whenever Delia tried to explore the secret of her cousin's actions, she returned from the adventure humiliated and abashed by the base motives she attributed to Charlotte. How was it that she, Delia Ralston, whose happiness had been open and avowed to the world, so often found herself denying poor Charlotte the secret of her scanted motherhood? She hated herself for this moment of envy whenever she detected it, and tried to atone for it by a softened manner and a more anxious consideration for Charlotte's feelings; but the attempt was not always successful, and Delia sometimes wondered if Charlotte did not resent any too open show of sympathy as an indirect glance at her misfortune. The worst of suffering such as hers was that it left one sore to the gentlest touch.[12]

Delia, slowly undressing before the same lace-draped toiletglass which had reflected her bridal image, was turning over these thoughts when she heard a faint knock on her door. On the threshold stood Tina in a dressing-gown, her dark curls falling over her shoulders. With a happy heartbeat Delia held out her arms.[13]

"I had to say good night, Mamma," the girl whispered.

"Of course, dear." Delia kissed her lifted forehead. "But run off now, or you might disturb your aunt. You know she sleeps badly, and you must be as quiet as a mouse now she's next to you."[14]

"Yes, I know," Tina acquiesced, with a grave glance that was almost of complicity.

She asked no further question; she did not linger; lifting Delia's hand, she held it a moment against her cheek, and then stole out as noiselessly as she had come.[15]

Chapter VIII

"But you must see," Charlotte Lovell insisted, laying aside the Evening *Post*,[1] "that Tina has changed. You do see that?"

The two women were sitting alone by the drawing-room fire in Gramercy Park. Tina had gone to dine with her cousin, Delia Halsey, and was to be taken afterward to a ball at the Vandergraves', from which the John Juniuses had promised to see her home. Mrs. Ralston and Charlotte, their early dinner finished, had the long evening to themselves. It was their custom, on such occasions, for Charlotte to read the news aloud to her cousin, while the latter embroidered; but tonight, all through Charlotte's conscientious progress from column to column, without a slip or an omission, Delia had felt her, for some special reason, alert to take advantage of her daughter's absence.[2]

To gain time, Mrs. Ralston bent over a dropped stitch[3] in her delicate white embroidery.

"Tina changed? Since when?" she questioned.

The answer flashed out instantly. "Since Lanning Halsey has been coming here so much."

"Lanning? I used to think he came for Delia," Mrs. Ralston mused, speaking at random to gain still more time.

"It's natural you should suppose that everyone came for Delia," Charlotte rejoined dryly; "but as Lanning continues to seek every chance of being with Tina—"[4]

———

Mrs. Ralston stole a swift glance at her cousin. She had in truth noticed that Tina had changed, as a flower changes at the mysterious moment when the unopened petals flush from within. The girl had grown handsomer, shyer, more silent, at times more irrelevantly gay. But Delia had not associated these variations of mood with the presence of Lanning Halsey, one of the numerous youths who had haunted the house before young Delia's marriage. There had, indeed, been a moment when Mrs. Ralston's eyes had been fixed, with a certain apprehension, on the handsome Lanning. Among all the sturdy and stolid Halsey cousins he was the only one to whom a prudent mother might have hesitated to intrust her daughter: it would have been hard to say why, except that he was handsomer and more talkative than the rest, chronically unpunctual, and totally unperturbed by the fact. Clem Spender had been like that; and what if young Delia—?[5]

But young Delia's mother was speedily reassured. The girl, herself arch and appetizing, took no interest in the corresponding graces except when backed by more solid qualities. A Ralston to the core, she demanded the Ralston virtues, and chose the Halsey most worthy of a Ralston bride.

Mrs. Ralston felt that Charlotte was waiting for her to speak. "It will be hard to get used to the idea of Tina's marrying," she said gently. "I don't know what we two old women shall do, alone[6] in this empty house—for it will be an empty house then. But I suppose we ought to face the idea."

"I *do* face it," said Charlotte Lovell gravely.

"And you dislike Lanning? I mean as a husband[7] for Tina?"

Miss Lovell folded the evening paper and stretched out a thin hand for her knitting. She glanced across the citron-wood worktable at her cousin. "Tina must not be too difficult—" she began.

"Oh—" Delia protested, reddening.

"Let us call things by their names," the other evenly pursued.

"That's my way, when I speak at all. Usually, as you know, I say nothing."

The widow made a sign of assent and Charlotte went on: "It's better so. But I've always known a time would come when we should have to talk things out."[8]

"Talk things out? You and I? What things?"[9]

"Tina's future."

There was a silence. Delia Ralston, who always responded instantly to the least appeal to her sincerity, breathed a deep sigh of relief. At last the ice in Charlotte's breast was breaking up!

"My dear," Delia murmured, "you know how much Tina's happiness concerns me. If you disapprove of Lanning Halsey as a husband, have you any other candidate in mind?"

Miss Lovell smiled one of her faint hard smiles. "I am not aware that there is a queue at the door. Nor do I disapprove of Lanning Halsey as a husband. Personally, I find him very agreeable:[10] I understand his attraction for Tina."

"Ah—Tina *is* attracted?"

"Yes."

Mrs. Ralston pushed aside her work and thoughtfully considered her cousin's sharply lined[11] face. Never had Charlotte Lovell more completely presented the typical image of the old maid than as she sat there, upright on her straight-backed chair, with narrowed elbows and clicking needles, and imperturbably discussed her daughter's marriage.

"I don't understand, Chatty. Whatever Lanning's faults are,— and I don't believe they're grave,—I share your liking for him. After all,"—Mrs. Ralston paused,—"what is it that people find so reprehensible in him? Chiefly, as far as I can hear, that he can't decide on the choice of a profession. The New York view about that is rather narrow, as we know. Young men may have other tastes—artistic— literary; they may even have difficulty in deciding."[12]

Both women colored slightly, and Delia guessed that the same reminiscence which shook her own bosom also throbbed under Charlotte's straitened[13] bodice.

Charlotte spoke. "Yes: I understand that. But hesitancy about a profession may cause hesitancy about—other decisions."[14]

"What do you mean? Surely not that Lanning—?"

"Lanning has not asked Tina to marry him."

"And you think he's hesitating?"[15]

———

Charlotte paused. The steady click of her needles punctuated the silence as once, years before, it had been punctuated by the tick of the Parisian clock on Delia's mantel. As Delia's memory fled back to that scene, she[16] felt its mysterious tension in the air.

Charlotte spoke. "Lanning is not hesitating any longer: he has decided not[17] to marry Tina. But he has also decided—not to give up seeing her."

Delia flushed abruptly:[18] she was irritated and bewildered by Charlotte's oracular phrases, doled out between parsimonious lips.

"You don't mean that he has offered himself and then drawn back? I can't think him capable of such an insult to Tina."

"He has not insulted Tina. He has simply told her that he can't afford to marry. Until he chooses a profession, his father will allow him only a few hundred dollars a year; and that may be suppressed, if—if he marries against his parents' wishes."[19]

It was Delia's turn to be silent. The past was too overwhelmingly resuscitated in Charlotte's words. Clement Spender stood before her, irresolute, impecunious, persuasive. Ah, if only she had let herself be persuaded!

"I'm very sorry that this should have happened to Tina. But as Lanning appears to have behaved honorably, and withdrawn without raising false expectations, we must hope—we must hope—"[20] Delia paused, not knowing what they must hope.

Charlotte Lovell laid down her knitting. "You know as well as I do, Delia, that every young man who is attracted by Tina will find as good reasons for not marrying her."

"Then you think his withdrawal[21] a pretext?"

"Naturally. The first of many that will be found by his successors—for of course he will have successors. Tina—attracts."

"Ah," Delia murmured.

Here they were at last face to face with the problem which, through all the years of silence and evasiveness, had lain as close to the surface as a body too hastily concealed![22] Delia drew another deep breath, which again was almost one of relief. She had always known that it would be difficult, almost impossible, to find a husband for Tina; and much as she desired Tina's happiness, some inmost selfishness whispered how much less lonely and purposeless the close of her own life would be should the girl be forced to share it. But how say this to Tina's mother?

"I hope you exaggerate, Charlotte. There may be disinterested characters. But in any case, surely[23] Tina need not be unhappy here, with us who love her so dearly."

"Tina an old maid? Never!" Charlotte Lovell rose abruptly, her closed hand crashing down on the slender work-table. "My child shall have her life,—her own life,—whatever it costs me."[24]

Delia's ready sympathy welled up. "I understand your feeling. I should want also—hard as it will be[25] to let her go. But surely there is no hurry—no reason for looking so far ahead. The child is not twenty. Wait."

Charlotte stood before her, motionless, perpendicular. At such moments she made Delia think of lava struggling through granite: there seemed no issue for the fires within.

"Wait? But if *she* doesn't wait?"

"But if he has withdrawn—what do you mean?"

"He has given up marrying her—but not seeing her."

Delia sprang up in her turn, flushed and trembling.

"Charlotte! Do you know what you are insinuating?"[26]

"Yes: I know."

"But it's too outrageous. No decent girl—"

The words died on Delia's lips. Charlotte Lovell held her eyes inexorably. "Girls are not always what you call decent," she declared.

Mrs. Ralston turned slowly back to her seat. Her tambour frame[27] had fallen to the floor: she stooped heavily to pick it up. Charlotte hung over her, relentless as doom.

"I can't imagine, Charlotte, what is gained by saying such things—even by hinting them. Surely you trust your own child—"28

Charlotte laughed. "My mother trusted me," she said.

"How dare you—how dare you?" Delia began; but her eyes fell, and she felt a tremor of weakness in her throat.

"Oh, I dare anything for Tina, even to judging her as she is," Tina's mother murmured.

"As she is? She's perfect."29

"Let us say, then, that she30 must pay for my imperfections. All I want is that she shouldn't pay too heavily."

Mrs. Ralston sat silent. It seemed to her that Charlotte spoke with the voice of all the dark destinies coiled under the safe surface of life; and that to such a voice there was no answer but an awed acquiescence.

"Poor Tina!" she breathed.

"Oh, I don't mean that she shall suffer! It's not for that that I've waited—waited.31 Only I've made mistakes: mistakes that I understand now, and must remedy. You've been too good to us—and we must go."

"Go?" Delia gasped.

"Yes. Don't think me ungrateful. You saved my child once—do you suppose I can forget? But now it's my turn—it's I who must save her. And it's only by taking her away from everything here—from everything she's known till now—that I can do it. She's lived too long among unrealities: and she's like me. They wont content her!"

"Unrealities?" Delia echoed vaguely.

"Unrealities for her. Young men who make love to her and can't marry her. Happy households where she's welcomed till she's suspected of designs on a brother or a husband—or else exposed to their insults. How could we ever have imagined, either of us, that the child could escape disaster? I thought only of her present happiness—of all the advantages, for both of us, of being with you. But this affair with young Halsey has opened my eyes. I must take Tina away. We must go and live somewhere where we're not known, where we shall be among plain people, leading plain lives.

Somewhere where she can find a husband, and make herself a home."

Charlotte paused. She had spoken in a rapid, monotonous tone, as if by rote; but now her voice broke, and she repeated painfully: "I'm not ungrateful."[32]

"Oh, don't let's speak of gratitude! What place has it between you and me?"[33]

———

Delia had risen and begun to move uneasily about the room. She longed to plead with Charlotte, to implore her not to be in haste, to picture to her the cruelty of severing Tina from all her habits and associations, of carrying her inexplicably away to lead "a plain life among plain people." What chance was there, indeed, that a creature so radiant could tamely submit[34] to such a fate, or find an acceptable husband in such conditions? The change might only precipitate a tragedy. Delia's experience was too limited for her to picture exactly what might happen to a girl like Tina, suddenly cut off from all that sweetened life for her; but vague visions of revolt and flight—of a "fall" deeper and more irretrievable than Charlotte's—flashed through her agonized imagination.

"It's too cruel—it's too cruel," she cried, speaking to herself rather than to Charlotte.

Charlotte, instead of answering, glanced abruptly at the clock.

"Do you know what time it is? Past midnight! I mustn't keep you sitting up for my foolish girl."

Delia's heart contracted. She saw that Charlotte wished to cut the conversation short, and to do so by reminding her that only Tina's mother had a right to decide what Tina's future should be. At that moment, though Delia had just protested that there could be no question of gratitude between them, Charlotte Lovell seemed to her a monster of ingratitude, and it was on the tip of her tongue to cry out: "Have all the years then given me no share in Tina?" But at the same instant she had put herself once more in Charlotte's place, and was feeling the mother's fierce terrors for her child. It was natural enough that Charlotte should resent the faintest attempt to usurp in private the authority she could never assert in public. With a pang of compassion Delia realized that she was literally the one being on earth before whom Charlotte could act the mother. "Poor thing—ah, let her!" she murmured inwardly.

"But why should you sit up for Tina? She has the key, and Delia is to bring her home."

Charlotte Lovell did not immediately answer. She rolled up her knitting, looked severely at one of the candelabra on the mantel-piece, and crossed over to straighten it. Then she picked up her work-bag.

"Yes, as you say—why should anyone sit up for her?" She moved about the room, blowing out the lamps, covering the fire, assuring herself that the windows were bolted, while Delia passively watched her. Then the cousins lighted their candles and walked up-stairs through the darkened house. Charlotte seemed determined to make no further allusion to the subject of their talk. On the landing she paused, bending her head toward Delia's nightly kiss.[35]

"I hope they've kept up your fire," she said, with her capable housekeeping air; and on Delia's hasty reassurance,[36] the two murmured a simultaneous "Good night," and Charlotte turned down the passage to her room.

CHAPTER IX

Delia's fire had been kept up, and her dressing-gown was warming on an armchair[1] near the hearth. But she neither undressed nor yet seated herself. Her conversation with Charlotte had filled her with a deep unrest.

For a few moments she stood in the middle of the floor, looking slowly about her. Nothing had ever been changed in the room which, even as a bride, she had planned to modernize. All her dreams of renovation had faded long ago. Some deep central indifference had gradually made her regard herself as a third person, living the life meant for another woman, a woman totally unrelated to the vivid Delia Lovell who had entered that house so full of plans and visions. The fault, she knew, was not her husband's. With a little managing and a little wheedling, she would have gained every point as easily as she had gained the capital one of taking the foundling baby under her wing. The difficulty was that, after that victory, nothing else seemed worth trying for. The first sight of little Tina had somehow decentralized Delia Ralston's whole life, making her indifferent to everything else, except indeed the welfare of her own husband and children. Ahead of her she saw only a future full of duties, and these she had gayly and faithfully accom-

plished. But her own life was over: she felt as detached as a cloistered nun.[2]

The change in her was too deep not to be visible. The Ralstons
openly gloried in dear Delia's conformity. Each acquiescence
passed for a concession, and their doctrine[3] was fortified by such
fresh proofs of its durability. Now, as Delia glanced about her at the
Leopold Robert lithographs, the family daguerreotypes, the rosewood and mahogany, she understood that she was looking at the
walls of her own grave.

The change had come on the day when Charlotte Lovell, cower-
ing on that very lounge, had made her terrible avowal. Then for the
first time Delia, with a kind of fearful exaltation, had heard the
blind forces of life groping and crying underfoot. But that day[4] also
she had known herself excluded from them, doomed to dwell
among shadows. Life had passed her by, and left her with the Ralstons.

Very well, then! She would make the best of herself, and of the
Ralstons. The vow was immediate and unflinching; and for nearly
twenty years she had gone on observing it. Once only had she
been, not a Ralston but herself; once only had it seemed worth
while. And now perhaps the same challenge had sounded again;
again, for a moment, it might be worth while to live. Not for the
sake of Clement Spender—poor Clement, married years ago to a
plain determined cousin, who had hunted him down in Rome, and
inclosing him in an unrelenting domesticity, had obliged all New
York on the grand tour[5] to buy his pictures with a resigned grimace.
No, not for Clement Spender, hardly for Charlotte or Tina, but for
her own sake, hers, Delia Ralston's, for the sake of her one missed
vision, her forfeited reality, she would once more break down the
Ralston barriers and reach out into the world.

A faint sound through the silent house disturbed Delia Ralston's
meditation. Listening, she heard Charlotte Lovell's door open, and
her stiff petticoats rustle toward the landing. A light glanced under
the door and vanished; Charlotte had passed the threshold on her
way downstairs.[6]

Without moving, Delia continued to listen. Perhaps the careful

Charlotte had gone down to make sure that the front door was not bolted, or that she had really covered up the fire. In that case,[7] her step would presently be heard returning. But no step sounded; and it became gradually evident that Charlotte had gone downstairs[8] to wait for her daughter. Why?

Delia's room was at the front of the house. She stole across the heavy carpet, drew aside the curtains and cautiously folded back the inner shutters. Below her lay the empty square, white with moonlight, its tree-trunks patterned on a fresh sprinkling of snow. The houses opposite slept in darkness: not a footstep broke the white surface; not a wheel-track marked the brilliant street. Overhead a heaven full of stars swam in the moonlight.[9]

——

Of the households around Gramercy Park Delia knew that only two others had gone to the ball: the Petrus Vandergraves and their cousins, the young Parmly Ralstons. The Lucius Lannings had just entered on their three years of mourning[10] for Mrs. Lucius' mother (it was hard on their daughter Kate, just eighteen, who would be unable to "come out" till she was twenty-one); young Mrs. Marcy Mingott was "expecting her third," and consequently secluded from the public eye for nearly a year; and the other denizens of the Square belonged to the undifferentiated and uninvited.

Delia pressed her forehead against the pane. Before long, carriages would turn the corner, and the sleeping square ring with hoof-beats; fresh laughter and young farewells would mount from the doorsteps. But why was Charlotte waiting for her daughter downstairs in the darkness?[11]

The Parisian clock struck one. Delia came back into the room, raked the fire, picked up a shawl, and wrapped in it, returned to her vigil. Ah, how old she must have grown, that she should feel the cold at such a moment! It reminded her of what the future held for her: neuralgia,[12] rheumatism, stiffness, accumulating infirmities. And never had she kept a moonlight watch with a lover's arms to warm her.

The square still lay silent. Yet the ball must surely be ending: the gayest dances did not last long after one in the morning, and the drive from University Place to Gramercy Park was a short one. Delia leaned in the embrasure and listened.

Hoof-beats sounded in Irving Place, and the Petrus Vandergraves' family coach drew up before the opposite house. The Vandergrave girls and their brother sprang out and mounted the steps; then the coach stopped a few doors farther on, and the Parmly Ralstons, brought home by their cousins, descended at their own door. The next carriage that rounded the corner must therefore be the John Juniuses, bringing Tina.[13]

—

The gilt clock struck half-past one. Delia wondered, knowing that young Delia, out of regard for John Junius' business hours, never stayed late at evening parties. Doubtless Tina had delayed her; Mrs. Ralston felt a little annoyed with Tina's thoughtlessness in keeping her cousin up. But the feeling was swept away by an immediate wave of sympathy. "We must go away somewhere, and lead plain lives among plain people." If Charlotte carried out her threat,—and Delia knew she would hardly have spoken unless her resolve had been taken.—it might be that at that very moment Tina was dancing her last *valse*.[14]

Another quarter of an hour passed; then, just as the cold was penetrating Delia's shawl, she saw two people turn into the deserted square from Irving Place. One was a young man in beaver hat and ample cloak. To his arm clung a feminine figure so closely wrapped and muffled that, until the corner light fell on it, Delia hesitated. After that, she wondered that she had not at once recognized Tina's dancing step, and her manner of tilting her head a little sideways to look up at the person she was talking to.[15]

Tina—Tina and Lanning Halsey, walking home alone in the small hours from the Vandergrave ball! Delia's first thought was of an accident: the carriage might have broken down, or her daughter been taken ill and obliged to return home. But no: in the latter case she would have sent the carriage on with Tina. And if there had been an accident of any sort, the young people would have been hastening to apprise Mrs. Ralston; instead of which, through the bitter brilliant night, they sauntered like lovers in a midsummer

glade, and Tina's thin slippers might have been treading daisies instead of snow.[16]

Delia began to tremble like a girl. In a flash she had the answer to
a question which had long been the subject of her secret conjec-
tures. How did lovers like Charlotte and Clement Spender contrive
to meet? What Latmian solitude[17] hid their clandestine joys? In the
exposed, compact little society to which they all belonged, how was
it possible, literally—for such things to happen? Delia would never
have dared to put the question to Charlotte; there were moments
when she almost preferred not to know, not even to hazard a guess.
But now, at a glance, she understood. How often Charlotte Lovell,
staying alone in town with her infirm grandmother, must have
walked home from evening parties with Clement Spender, how
often have let herself and him into the darkened house in Mercer
Street, where there was no one to spy upon their coming but a deaf
old lady and her aged servants, all securely sleeping overhead.
Delia, at the thought, saw the grim drawing-room which had been
their moonlit forest, the drawing-room into which old Mrs. Lovell
no longer descended, with its swathed chandelier and hard Empire
sofas,[18] and the blank-faced caryatids[19] of the mantel; she pictured
the shaft of moonlight falling across the swans and garlands of the
pompous carpet, and in that icy light two young figures in each
other's arms.[20]

———

Yes. It must have been some such memory that had roused Charlotte's suspicions, excited her fears, sent her down in the darkness
to confront the culprits. Delia shivered at the irony of the con-
frontation. If Tina had but known! But to Tina, of course, Charlotte was still what she had long since resolved to be: the image of
prudish spinsterhood. And Delia could imagine how quietly and
decently the scene below stairs would presently be enacted: no as-
tonishment, no reproaches, no insinuations, but a smiling and reso-
lute ignoring of excuses.

"What, Tina? You walked home with Lanning? You imprudent
child—in this wet snow! Ah, I see: Delia was worried about the
baby, and ran off early, promising to send back the carriage—and it

never came? Well, my dear, I congratulate you on finding Lanning to see you home. . . . . Yes—I sat up because I couldn't for the life of me remember whether you'd taken the latchkey—was there ever such a flighty old aunt? But don't tell your mamma, dear, or she'd scold me for being so forgetful, and for staying downstairs in the cold. . . . . You're quite sure you have the key? Ah, Lanning has it? Thank you, Lanning—so kind. Good night—or one really ought to say, good morning!"[21]

As Delia reached this point in her mute representation of Charlotte's monologue, the front door slammed below, and young Lanning Halsey walked slowly away across the square. Delia saw him pause on the opposite pavement, look up at the unlit house-front, and then turn lingeringly away. His dismissal had taken exactly as long as Delia had calculated it would. A moment later she saw a passing light under her door, heard the starched rustle of Charlotte's petticoats, and knew that mother and daughter had reached their rooms.[22]

Slowly, with stiff motions, she began to undress, blew out her candles, and knelt long by her bedside,[23] her face hidden.

Chapter X

Lying awake till morning, Delia lived over every detail of the fateful day when she had assumed the charge of Charlotte's child. At the time she had been hardly more than a child herself, and then there had been no one for her to turn to, no one to fortify her resolution, or to advise her how to put it into effect. Since then, the accumulated experiences of seventeen years ought to have prepared her for emergencies, and taught her to advise others instead of seeking their guidance. But these years of experience weighed on her like chains binding her down to her narrow plot of life: independent action struck her as more dangerous, less conceivable, than when she had first ventured on it. There seemed to be so many more people to "consider" now ("consider" was the Ralston word): her children, their children, the families into which they had married. What would the Halseys say, and what the Ralstons? Had she then become a Ralston through and through?[1]

A few hours later she sat in old Dr. Lanskell's library, her eyes on his sooty Smyrna rug.[2] Dr. Lanskell no longer practiced: at most, he went to a few old patients, gave consultations in "difficult" cases. But he remained a power in his own kingdom, a sort of lay pope or medical elder, to whom the patients he had healed of physical ills now returned for moral medicine. People were agreed that Dr. Lanskell's judgment was sound; but what secretly drew them to him was the fact that, in the most totem-ridden[3] of communities, he was known not to be afraid of anything.

Now, as Delia sat by his grate, and watched his massive silver-headed figure moving ponderously about the room, between rows of calf bindings, and the Dying Gladiators and Young Augustuses[4] of grateful patients, she already felt the reassurance communicated by his mere bodily presence.

"You see, when I first took Tina, I didn't perhaps consider sufficiently—"

The Doctor halted behind his desk and brought his fist down on it in a genial thump. "Thank God you didn't! There are considerers enough in this town without you, Delia Lovell."[5]

She looked up quickly. "Why do you call me Delia Lovell?"

"Well, because today I rather suspect you *are*," he rejoined astutely; and she met this with a wistful laugh.

"Perhaps, if I hadn't been, once before—I mean, if I'd always been a prudent deliberate Ralston, it[6] would have been kinder to Tina in the end."

Dr. Lanskell sank his gouty bulk[7] into the chair behind his desk, and beamed at her through ironic spectacles.[8] "I hate in-the-end kindnesses: they're about as nourishing as the third day of cold mutton."

She pondered. "Of course, I realize that if I adopt Tina—"

"Yes?"

"Well, people will say—"[9] A deep blush rose to her throat, covered her cheeks and brow, and ran like fire under her decently parted hair.

He nodded: "Yes."

"Or else"[10]—the blush darkened—"that she's Jim's—"

Again Dr. Lanskell nodded. "That's what they're more likely to think; and what's the harm if they do? I know Jim: he asked no questions when you took the child—but he knew whose she was."

She raised astonished eyes. "He knew?"[11]

"Yes: he came to me. And—well—in the baby's interest,[12] I violated professional secrecy. That's how Tina got a home. You're not going to denounce me, are you?"

"Oh, Dr. Lanskell!"[13] Her eyes filled with painful tears. "Jim knew? And didn't tell me?"

"No. People didn't tell each other things much in those days, did they? But he admired you enormously for what you did. And if you assume—as I suppose you do—that he's now in a world of completer enlightenment, why not take it for granted that he'll admire you still more for what you're going to do? Presumably," the Doctor concluded sardonically, "people realize in heaven that it's a devilish sight harder, on earth, to do a brave thing at fifty[14] than at twenty-five."

"Ah, that's what I was thinking this morning," she confessed.

"Well, you're going to prove the contrary this afternoon." He looked at his watch, stood up and laid a fatherly hand on her shoulder. "Let people think what they choose; and send young Delia to me if she gives you any trouble. Your boy wont, you know, nor John Junius either; it must have been a woman who invented that third-and-fourth-generation idea."[15]

An elderly maidservant[16] looked in, and Delia rose; but on the threshold she halted.

"I have an idea it's Charlotte I may have to send to you."

"Charlotte?"

"She'll hate what I'm going to do, you know."

Dr. Lanskell lifted his silver eyebrows.[17] "Yes: poor Charlotte! I suppose she's jealous? That's where the truth of the third-and-fourth-generation business comes in, after all. Somebody always has to foot the bill."

"Ah—if only Tina doesn't!"

"Well—that's just what Charlotte will come to recognize.[18] So your course is clear."

He guided her out through the brown dining-room,[19] where some poor people and one or two old patients were already waiting.

—

Delia's course, in truth, seemed clear enough till, that afternoon, she summoned Charlotte alone to her bedroom. Tina was lying down with a headache: it was the accepted attitude[20] of young ladies in sentimental dilemmas, and greatly simplified the communion of their elders.

Delia and Charlotte had exchanged only conventional phrases over their midday meal; but Delia had the sense that her cousin's resolution was definitely taken. The events of the previous evening had evidently confirmed Charlotte's view that the time had come for decisive measures.[21]

Miss Lovell, closing the bedroom door with her dry deliberateness, advanced toward the chintz lounge between the windows.

"You wanted to see me, Delia?"

"Yes. —Oh, don't sit there," Mrs. Ralston exclaimed uncontrollably.

———

Charlotte stared: was it possible that she did not remember the sobs of anguish she had once smothered in those cushions?[22]

"Not—"[23]

"No; come nearer.[24] Sometimes I think I'm a little deaf," Delia nervously explained, pushing a chair up to her own.

"Ah!" Charlotte seated herself. "I hadn't remarked it. But if you are, it may have saved you from hearing at what hour of the morning Tina came back from the Vandergraves.[25] She would never forgive herself—inconsiderate as she is—if she thought she'd waked you."

"She didn't wake me," Delia answered. Inwardly she thought: "Charlotte's mind is made up; I sha'n't be able to move her."

"I suppose Tina enjoyed herself very much at the ball?" she continued.

"Well, she's paying for it with a sick headache.[26] Such excitements are not meant for her. I've already told you—"

"Yes," Mrs. Ralston interrupted. "It's to continue our talk that I've asked you to come up this afternoon."[27]

"To continue it?" The brick-red circles appeared in Charlotte's dried cheeks. "Is it worth while? I think I ought to tell you at once that my mind's made up. You must recognize that I know what's best for Tina."[28]

"Yes; of course. But wont you at least allow me a share in your decision?"

"A share?"

Delia leaned forward, laying a warm hand on her cousin's interlocked fingers. "Charlotte, once in this room you asked me[29] to help you—you believed I could. Wont you believe it again?"

Charlotte's lips grew rigid. "I believe the time has come for me to help myself."

"At the cost of Tina's happiness?"

"No; but to spare her greater unhappiness."

"But Charlotte.[30] Tina's happiness is all I want."

"Oh, I know. You've done all you could do for my child."

"No, not all."[31] Delia rose, and stood before her cousin with a kind of solemnity. "But now I'm going to." It was as if she had pronounced a vow.

Charlotte looked up with a glitter of apprehension in her eyes.[32]

"If you mean that you're going to use your influence with the Halseys—I'm very grateful to you; I shall always be grateful. But I don't want a compulsory marriage for my child."

Delia flushed at the other's incomprehension. It seemed to her that her purpose[33] must be written on her face. "I'm going to adopt Tina—give her my name," she said.

Charlotte stared[34] at her stonily. "Adopt her—adopt her?"

"Don't you see, dear, the difference it will make? There's my mother's money—the Lovell money; it is not much, to be sure; but Jim always wanted it to go back to my family. And my Delia and her brother are so handsomely provided for. There's no reason why my little fortune shouldn't go to Tina—and why she shouldn't be known as Tina Ralston." Delia paused. "I believe—I think I know—that Jim would have approved of that too."[35]

"Approved?"

"Yes. Can't you see that when he let me take the child, he must have foreseen and accepted whatever—might come of it?"[36]

Charlotte stood up also. "Thank you, Delia. But nothing more must come of it, except our leaving you—our leaving[37] you now. I'm sure that's what Jim would have approved."

—

Mrs. Ralston drew back a step or two. Charlotte's cold resolution benumbed her courage, and she could find no immediate reply.

"Ah, then it's easier for you to sacrifice Tina's happiness than your pride?"[38]

"My pride? I've no right to any pride, except in my child. And that I'll never sacrifice."

"No one asks you to. You're not reasonable. You're cruel. All I want is to be allowed to help Tina, and you speak as if I were interfering with your rights."

"My rights?" Charlotte caught her up again.[39] "What are they? I have no rights, either before the law or in the heart of my own child."

"How can you say such things? You know how Tina loves you."

"Yes—compassionately, as I used to love[40] my old-maid aunts. There were two of them—you remember? Like withered babies! We children used to be warned never to say anything that might shock Aunt Josie or Aunt Nonie, exactly as I heard you telling Tina the other night—"

"Oh—" Delia murmured.

Charlotte Lovell stood before her, haggard, rigid, unrelenting. "No, it's gone on long enough. I mean to tell her everything—[41] and to take her away."

"To tell her about her birth?"

"I was never ashamed of it," Charlotte panted.

"You sacrifice[42] her, then—sacrifice her to your desire for mastery?"

The two women faced each other, both with weapons spent. Delia, through the tremor of her own indignation, saw her antagonist slowly waver, step backward, sink down with a broken murmur on the lounge. Charlotte hid her face in the cushions, clenching them with violent hands. The same fierce maternal passion that had once flung her down upon those same cushions was now bowing her still lower, in the throes of a bitterer renunciation. Delia seemed to hear again the old cry: "But how can I give up my baby?" Her own momentary resentment melted, and she bent over the mother's laboring[43] shoulders.

"Chatty—it wont be like giving her up this time. Can't we just go on loving her together?"

Charlotte did not answer. For a long time she lay silent, immovable, her face hidden: she seemed to fear to turn it to the face bent down to her. But presently Delia was aware of a gradual relaxing of the stretched muscles, and saw that one of her cousin's hands was stirring[44] and groping. She lowered her hand to the seeking fingers, and it was caught and pressed to Charlotte's lips.

Chapter XI

Tina Lovell—now Miss Clementina Ralston—was to be married in July to Lanning Halsey. The engagement had been announced only in the previous April; and the female elders of the tribe had begun by crying out against the indelicacy of so brief a betrothal.[1] It was unanimously agreed in New York that "young people should be given the time to get to know each other;" and though the greater number of the couples constituting New York society had played together as children, and been born of parents as long and as familiarly acquainted, yet some mysterious law of decorum required that the newly affianced should always be regarded as being also newly acquainted. In the Southern States things were differently conducted: headlong engagements, even runaway marriages, were not uncommon in the annals of Virginia and Maryland; but such rashness was less consonant with the sluggish blood of New York, where the pace of life was still set with a Dutch deliberateness.

In a case as unusual as Tina Ralston's, however, it was hardly surprising that tradition had been disregarded. In the first place, everyone knew that she was no more Tina Ralston than you or I—unless, indeed, one were to credit the rumors about poor Jim's unsuspected "past," and his widow's magnanimity. But the opinion of the majority was against this. People were reluctant to charge a dead man with an offense from which he could not clear himself; and the Ralstons unanimously declared that, thoroughly as they disapproved of Mrs. James Ralston's action, they were convinced that she would not have adopted Tina had her doing so appeared to "cast a slur" on her late husband's morals.[2]

No: the girl was perhaps a Lovell,—though even that idea was not generally held,—but she was certainly not a Ralston. Her black eyes and flighty ways too obviously excluded her from the clan for any formal excommunication to be pronounced against her. In fact, most people believed that—as Dr. Lanskell had always affirmed—her origin was really undiscoverable, that she represented one of the unsolved mysteries which occasionally perplex and irritate well-regulated societies, and that her adoption by Delia Ralston was simply one more proof of the Lovell clannishness, since the child had been taken in by Mrs. Ralston only because her cousin Charlotte was so attached to it. To say that Mrs. Ralston's son and daughter were pleased with the idea of Tina's adoption would have been an exaggeration; but they abstained from comment, minimizing the effect of their mother's whim by a dignified silence. It was the old New York way for families thus to screen the eccentricities of an individual member, and where there was "money enough to go around," the heirs would have been thought vulgarly grasping to protest at the alienation of a small sum from the general inheritance.[3]

Nevertheless, Delia Ralston, from the moment of Tina's adoption, was perfectly aware of a different attitude on the part of her children. They dealt with her patiently, almost paternally, as with a minor in whom one juvenile lapse has been condoned, but who must be subjected, in consequence, to a stricter vigilance; and society treated her in the same indulgent but guarded manner.

She had (it was Sillerton Jackson who first phrased it) an undoubted way of "carrying things off," since Mrs. Manson Mingott had broken her husband's will, nothing like it had been seen in New York. But Mrs. Ralston's method was different, and less easy to analyze. What Mrs. Manson Mingott had accomplished with epigram, invective, insistency and runnings to and fro, the other achieved without raising her voice or seeming to take a step from the beaten path. When she had persuaded Jim Ralston to take in the foundling baby, it had been done in the turn of a hand, one didn't know when or how; and the next day he and she were as untroubled and beaming as usual. And now, this adoption! Well, she had pursued the same method; as Sillerton Jackson said, she behaved as if her adopting Tina had always been an understood thing, as if she wondered that people should wonder. And in face of her wonder, theirs seemed foolish, and they gradually desisted.[4]

In reality, behind Delia's assurance there was a tumult of doubts and uncertainties. But she had once learned that one can do almost anything (perhaps even murder) if one does not attempt to explain it; and the lesson had never been forgotten. She had never explained the taking over of the foundling baby; nor was she now going to explain its adoption. She was just going about her business as if nothing had happened that needed to be accounted for; and a long inheritance of moral modesty helped her to keep her questionings to herself.

These questionings were in fact less concerned with public opinion than with Charlotte Lovell's private thoughts. Charlotte, after her first moment of tragic resistance, had shown herself pathetically, almost painfully, grateful. That she had reason to be, Tina's attitude abundantly revealed. Tina, during the first days after her return from the Vandergrave ball, had shown a closed and darkened face that terribly reminded Delia of the ghastliness of Charlotte Lovell's sudden reflection, years before, in her own bedroom mirror. The first chapter of the mother's history was already written in the daughter's eyes; and the Spender blood in Tina might well precipitate the sequence. In those few hours of silent observation Delia perceived, with terror and compassion, the justification of Charlotte's misgivings. The girl had nearly been lost to them both: at all costs such a risk must not be renewed.[5]

The Halseys, on the whole, had behaved, admirably. Lanning wished to marry dear Delia Ralston's protégée—who was shortly, it was understood, to take her adopted mother's name, and inherit her fortune. To what more could a Halsey aspire than one more alliance with a Ralston? The families had always intermarried. The Halsey parents gave their blessing with a precipitation which made it evident that they too had their anxieties, and that the relief of seeing Lanning "settled" would more than compensate for the conceivable drawbacks of the marriage—though, once it was decided on, they would not admit such drawbacks existed. For old New York always thought away whatever interfered with the perfect propriety of its arrangements.[6]

Charlotte Lovell of course perceived and recognized all this. She accepted the situation—in her private hours with Delia—as one more in the long list of mercies bestowed on an undeserving sinner. And one phrase of hers perhaps gave the clue to her acceptance: "Now at least she'll never suspect the truth." It had come to be the poor creature's ruling purpose that her child should never guess the tie between them.[7]

But Delia's chief support was the sight of Tina. The older woman, whose whole life had been shaped and colored by the faint reflection of a rejected happiness, hung dazzled in the light of bliss accepted. Sometimes, as she watched Tina's changing face, she felt as though her own blood were beating in it, as though she could read every thought and emotion feeding those tumultuous currents. Tina's love was a stormy affair, with endless ups and downs of rapture and depression, arrogance and self-abasement; Delia saw displayed before her, with an artless frankness, all the visions, cravings and imaginings of her own stifled youth.[8]

What the girl really thought of her adoption it was not easy to discover. She had been given, at fourteen, the current version of her origin, and had accepted it as carelessly as a happy child accepts some remote and inconceivable fact that does not alter the familiar order of things. And she accepted her adoption in the same spirit. She knew that the name of Ralston had been given to her to facilitate her marriage with Lanning Halsey; and Delia had the impression that all irrelevant questionings were submerged in an overwhelming gratitude. "I've always thought of you as my mamma; and now, you dearest, you really are," she had whispered, her cheek against Delia's; and Delia had laughed back: "Well, if the lawyers can make me so!" But there the matter dropped, swept away on the current of Tina's bliss. They were all, in those days—Delia, Charlotte, even the gallant Lanning—rather like straws whirling about on a sunlit torrent.[9]

The golden flood swept them onward, nearer and nearer to the enchanted date; and Delia, deep in bridal preparations, wondered at the comparative indifference with which she had ordered and inspected her own daughter's twelve-dozen-of-everything. There had been nothing to quicken the pulse in young Delia's placid bridal; but as Tina's wedding-day approached, imagination bourgeoned like the year. The wedding was to be celebrated at Lovell Place, the old house on the Sound where Delia Lovell had herself been married, and where, since her mother's death, she spent her summers. Although the neighborhood was already overspread with a network of mean streets,[10] the old house, with its thin colonnaded veranda, still looked across an uncurtailed lawn and leafy shrubberies to the narrows of Hell Gate;[11] and the drawing-rooms kept their frail, slender settees, their Sheraton consoles and cabinets.[12] It had been thought useless to discard them for more fashionable furniture, since the growth of the city made it certain that the place must eventually be sold.[13]

Tina, like Mrs. Ralston, was to have a "house-wedding," though Episcopalian society was beginning to disapprove of such ceremonies, which were regarded as the despised *pis aller*[14] of Baptists, Methodists, Unitarians and the other altarless sects. In Tina's case, however, both Delia and Charlotte felt that the greater privacy of a marriage in the house made up for its more secular character; and the Halseys discreetly favored their decision. The ladies accordingly settled themselves at Lovell Place before the end of June, and every morning young Lanning Halsey's cat-boat[15] was seen beating across the bay, and furling its sail at the anchorage below the lawn.

—

There had never been a fairer June in anyone's memory. The damask roses and mignonette[16] below the veranda had never sent such a breath of summer through the tall French windows; the gnarled orange-trees[17] brought out from the old arcaded orange-house had never been so thickly blossomed; the very haycocks[18] on the lawn gave out whiffs of Araby.[19]

The day before the wedding Delia Ralston sat on the veranda watching the moon rise across the Sound. She was tired with the multitude of last preparations, and sad at the thought of Tina's going. On the following evening the house would be empty; till death came, she and Charlotte would sit alone together beside the evening lamp. Such repinings were foolish—they were, she reminded herself, "not like her." But too many memories stirred and murmured in her: her heart was haunted. As she closed the door on the silent drawing-room,—already transformed into a chapel, with its lace-hung altar, the tall alabaster vases awaiting their white roses and June lilies, the strip of red carpet dividing the rows of chairs from door to chancel,—she felt that it had been a mistake to come back to Lovell Place for the wedding. She saw herself again, in her high-waisted "India mull"[20] embroidered with daisies, her satin sandals, her Brussels veil[21]—saw again her reflection in the sallow pier-glass,[22] as she had entered that same room on Jim Ralston's triumphant arm, and the one terrified glance she had exchanged with her own image before she took her stand under the bell of white roses, and smiled upon the congratulating company. Ah, what a different image the pier-glass would reflect tomorrow![23]

Charlotte Lovell's brisk step sounded in the hall, and she came out and joined Mrs. Ralston.

"I've been to the kitchen to tell Melissa Grimes that she'd better count on two hundred plates[24] of ice-cream."

"Two hundred? Yes—I suppose she had, with all the Philadelphia connection coming." Delia pondered. "How about the doylies?"[25] she inquired.

"With your aunt Cecilia Vandergrave's we shall manage beautifully."

"Yes. . . . . Thank you,[26] Charlotte, for taking all this trouble."

"Oh—" Charlotte protested, with her flitting sneer; and Delia perceived the irony of thanking a mother for occupying herself with the details of her own daughter's wedding.

"Do sit down, Chatty," she murmured, feeling herself redden at her blunder.[27]

———

Charlotte, with a sigh, sat down on the nearest chair.

"We shall have a beautiful day tomorrow," she said, pensively surveying the placid heaven.

"Yes. Where is Tina?"

"She was very tired. I've sent her upstairs to lie down."

This seemed so eminently suitable that Delia made no immediate answer. After an interval she said: "We shall miss her."

Charlotte's reply was an inarticulate murmur.

The two cousins remained silent, Charlotte as usual bolt upright, her thin hands clutched on the arms of her old-fashioned rush-bottomed seat, Delia somewhat heavily sunk into the depths of a high-backed armchair. The two had exchanged their last remarks on the preparations for the morrow,[28] and nothing more remained to be said as to the number of guests, the brewing of the punch, the arrangements for the robing of the clergy, and the disposal of the presents in the best spare-room.

———

Only one subject had not yet been touched on, and Delia, as she watched her cousin's profile grimly cut upon the melting twilight, waited for Charlotte to speak. But Charlotte remained silent.

"I have been thinking," Delia at length began, a slight tremor in her voice, "that I ought presently—"

She fancied she saw Charlotte's hands tighten on the knobs of the chair-arms.

"You ought presently—?"

"Well, before Tina goes to bed, perhaps go up for a few minutes—"

Charlotte remained silent, visibly resolved on making no effort to assist her.

"Tomorrow," Delia continued, "we shall be in such a rush from the earliest moment that I don't see how, in the midst of all the interruptions and excitement, I can possibly——"[29]

"Possibly?" Charlotte monotonously echoed.

Delia felt her blush deepening through the dusk. "Well, I suppose you agree with me that a word ought to be said to the child as to the new duties and responsibilities that—well—what is usual, in fact, at such a time," she falteringly ended.[30]

"Yes, I have thought of that," Charlotte answered abruptly. She said no more, but Delia divined in her the stirring of that obscure opposition which, in the crucial moments of Tina's life, seemed automatically to manifest itself. She could not understand why Charlotte should at times grow so enigmatic and inaccessible, but she saw no reason why this change of mood should interfere with what she deemed to be her own duty. Tina must long for her guiding hand into the new life as much as she yearned for the exchanges of half-confidences which would be her real farewell to her adopted daughter. Her heart beating a little more quickly than usual, she rose and walked through the open window into the shadowy drawing-room. The moon, between the columns of the veranda, sent a broad light across the rows of chairs, irradiated the lace-decked altar with its empty candlesticks and vases, and outlined with silver Delia's heavy reflection in the pier-glass.[31]

—

She crossed the room toward the hall.

"Delia!" Charlotte's voice sounded behind her. She turned, and the two women faced each other in the revealing light. Charlotte's face looked as it had looked on the dreadful day when Delia had suddenly seen it in the glass above her shoulder.[32]

"You were going up now—to speak[33] to Tina?" Charlotte asked.

"I—yes. It's nearly nine. I thought—"[34]

"Yes; I understand." Miss Lovell made a visible effort at self-control. "Please understand me too, Delia, if I ask you—not to."

"Not to?" Delia scrutinized her[35] cousin with a vague sense of apprehension. What mystery did this strange request conceal? But no—such a doubt as flitted across her mind was inadmissible. She was too sure of her Tina!

"I confess I don't understand you, Charlotte.[36] You surely feel that, on the night before her wedding, a girl ought to have a mother's counsel, a mother's—"

"Yes: I feel that." Charlotte Lovell took a hurried breath. "But the question is: which of us is her mother?"[37]

Delia drew back involuntarily. "Which of us?"[38] she stammered.

"Yes. Oh, don't imagine it's the first time I've asked myself the question! There—I mean to be calm, quite calm. I don't intend to go back to the past. I've accepted—accepted everything—Gratefully. Only tonight—just tonight."[39]

Delia felt the rush of pity that always[40] prevailed over every other feeling in her rare interchanges of truth with Charlotte Lovell. Her throat filled with tears, and she remained silent.

"Just tonight," Charlotte concluded, "*I'm* her mother."

"Charlotte! You're not going to tell her so—not now?" broke involuntarily from Delia.

Charlotte gave a faint laugh. "If I did, should you hate it as much as all that?"

"Hate it? What a word, between us!"

"Between us? But it's been between us[41] since the beginning—the very beginning! Since the day when you discovered that Clement Spender hadn't quite broken his heart because he wasn't good enough for you, since you found your revenge and your triumph in keeping me at your mercy and in taking his child from me!" Charlotte's words flamed up as if from the depth of the infernal fires; then the blaze dropped, her head sank forward, and she stood before Delia dumb and stricken.

Delia's first movement was one of an indignant recoil. Where she had felt only tenderness, compassion, the impulse to help and befriend, these darknesses had been smoldering[42] in the other's breast! It was as if a poisonous smoke had swept over some pure summer landscape.

———

Usually such feelings were quickly followed by a reaction of sympathy. But now she felt none. An utter weariness possessed her.

"Yes," she said slowly, "I sometimes believe you really have hated me from the very first, hated[43] me for everything I've tried to do for you."

Charlotte raised her head sharply. "To do for me? But everything you've done has been done for Clement Spender!"

Delia stared at her with a kind of terror. "You are horrible, Charlotte. Upon my honor, I haven't thought of Clement Spender for years."

"Ah, but you have—you have! You've always thought of him in thinking of Tina—of him and nobody else! A woman never stops thinking of the man she loves. She thinks of him years afterward, in all sorts of unconscious ways, in thinking of all sorts of things—books, pictures, sunsets, a flower or a ribbon—or a clock on the mantelpiece." Charlotte broke off with her sneering laugh. "That was what I gambled on, you see—that's why I came to you that day. I knew I was giving Tina another mother."

Again the poisonous smoke seemed to envelope[44] Delia: that she and Charlotte, two spent old women, should be standing before Tina's bridal altar and talking to each other of hatred, seemed unimaginably hideous and degrading.

"You wicked woman—you *are* wicked!" she exclaimed.

Then the evil mist cleared away, and through it she saw the baffled pitiful figure of the mother who was not a mother, and who, for every benefit accepted, felt herself robbed of a privilege. She moved nearer to Charlotte and laid a hand on her arm.

"Not here! Don't let us talk like this here."

The other drew away from her. "Wherever you please, then. I'm not particular!"

"But tonight, Charlotte—the night before Tina's wedding? Isn't every place in this house full of her? How could we go on saying cruel things to each other anywhere?" Charlotte was silent, and Delia continued in a steadier voice: "Nothing you say can really hurt me—for long; and I don't want to hurt you—I never did."

"You tell me that—and you've left nothing undone to divide me from my daughter! Do you suppose it's been easy, all these years, to hear her call you mother? Oh, I know, I know—it was agreed that she must never guess. But if you hadn't perpetually come between us, she'd have had no one but me, she'd have felt about me as a child feels about its mother, she'd have had to love me better than anyone else. With all your forbearances and your generosities, you've ended by robbing me of my child. And I've put up with it all for her sake—because I knew I had to. But tonight—tonight she belongs to me. Tonight I can't bear that she should call you mother."[45]

Delia Ralston made no immediate reply. It seemed to her that for the first time she had sounded the deepest depths of maternal passion, and she stood awed at the echoes it gave back.

"How you must love her—to say such things to me!" she murmured; and then,[46] with a final effort: "Yes, you're right. I wont go up to her. It's you who must go."

Charlotte started toward her impulsively; but with a hand lifted as if in defense, Delia moved across the room and out again to the veranda. As she sank down in her chair, she heard the drawing-room door open and close, and the sound of Charlotte's feet on the stairs.[47]

———

Delia sat alone in the night. The last drop of her magnanimity had been spent, and she tried to avert her shuddering mind from Charlotte. What was happening at this moment upstairs? With what dark revelations were Tina's bridal dreams to be defaced? Well, that was not matter for conjecture, either. She, Delia Ralston, had played her part, done her utmost: there remained nothing now but to try to lift her spirit above the embittering sense of failure.

There was a strange element of truth in some of the things that Charlotte had said. With what divination that maternal passion[48] had endowed her! Her jealousy seemed to have a million feelers. Yes; it was true that the sweetness and peace of Tina's bridal eve had been filled, for Delia, with visions of her own unrealized past. Softly, imperceptibly, it had reconciled her to the memory of what she had missed. All these last days she had been living the girl's life, she had been Tina, and Tina had been her own girlish self, the far-off Delia Lovell. Now, for the first time, without shame, without self-reproach, without a pang or a scruple, Delia could yield to that vision of requited love from which her imagination had always turned away. She had made her choice in youth, and she had accepted it in maturity; and here in this bridal joy, so mysteriously her own, was the compensation for all she had missed and yet never renounced.

Delia understood now that Charlotte had guessed all this, and that the knowledge had filled her with a fierce resentment. Charlotte had said long ago that Clement Spender had never really belonged to her; now she had perceived that it was the same with Clement Spender's child. As the truth stole upon Delia, her heart[49] melted with the old compassion for Charlotte. She saw that it was a terrible, a sacrilegious thing, to interfere with another's destiny, to lay the tenderest touch upon any human being's right to love and suffer after his own fashion. Delia had twice intervened in Charlotte Lovell's life: it was natural that Charlotte should be her enemy. If only she did not revenge herself by wounding Tina!

The adopted mother's thoughts reverted painfully to the little white room upstairs. She had meant her half-hour with Tina to leave the girl with thoughts as fragrant as the flowers she was to find beside her when she woke. And now—

Delia started up from her musing. There was a step on the stair—Charlotte coming down through the silent house. Delia stood up[50] with a vague impulse of escape: she felt that she could not face her cousin's eyes. She turned the corner of the veranda, hoping to find the shutters of the dining-room unlatched, and to slip away unnoticed to her room; but in a moment Charlotte was beside her.

"Delia!"

"Ah, it's you? I was going up to bed." For the life of her Delia could not keep an edge of hardness from her voice.

"Yes: it's late. You must be very tired." Charlotte paused: her own voice was strained and painful.

"I *am* tired," Delia acknowledged.

In the moonlit hush the other went up to her, laying a timid touch on her arm.

"Not till you've seen Tina."

Delia stiffened. "Tina? But it's late! Isn't she sleeping? I thought you'd stay with her until—"

"I don't know if she's sleeping." Charlotte paused. "I haven't been in—but there's a light under her door."

"You haven't been in?"

"No: I just stood in the passage, and tried—"

"Tried—?"

"To think of something—something to say to her without—without her guessing."[51] A sob stopped her, but she pressed on with a final effort. "It's no use. You were right: there's nothing I can say. You're her real mother. Go to her. It's not your fault—or mine."

"Oh—" Delia cried.

Charlotte clung to her in inarticulate abasement. "You said I was wicked—I'm not wicked. After all, she was mine when she was little!"

Delia put an arm about her shoulder.

"Hush, dear! We'll go to her together."

The other yielded automatically to her touch, and side by side the two women mounted the stairs, Charlotte timing her impetuous step to Delia's stiffened movements. They walked down the passage to Tina's door; but there Charlotte Lovell paused and shook her head.

"No—you," she whispered suddenly,[52] and turned away.

—

Tina lay in bed, her arms folded under her head, her happy eyes reflecting the silver space of sky that filled[53] the window. She smiled at Delia through her dream.

"I knew you'd come."

Delia sat down beside her, and their clasped hands lay upon the coverlet. They did not say much, after all; or else their communion had no need of words. Delia never knew how long she sat by the child's side: she abandoned herself to the spell of the moonlit hour.

But suddenly she thought of Charlotte, alone behind the shut door of her own room, watching, struggling, listening. Delia must not, for her own pleasure, prolong that tragic vigil. She bent down to kiss Tina good night;[54] then she paused on the threshold and turned back.

"Darling! Just one thing more."

"Yes?" Tina murmured.[55]

"I want you to promise me—"

"Everything, everything, you darling!"[56]

"Well, then, that when you go away tomorrow—at the very last moment, you understand—"

"Yes?"

"After you've said good-by to me, and to everybody else—just as Lanning helps you into the carriage—"

"Yes?"

"That you'll give your last kiss to Aunt Charlotte. Don't forget—the very last."

NOTES

In addition to various Internet sources, the Oxford English Dictionary, *and various encyclopedias, I consulted the following sources:*

Frye, Northrop. The Secular Scripture: A Study of the Structure of Romance. *Cambridge: Harvard University Press, 1976.*

Lewis, R.W.B. Edith Wharton: A Biography. *New York: Harper & Row, 1975.*

———*and Nancy Lewis, eds.* The Letters of Edith Wharton. *New York: Scribner's, 1988.*

Wright, Sarah Bird. Edith Wharton A to Z: The Essential Guide to the Life and Work. *New York: Facts on File, 1998.*

Yalom, Marilyn. A History of the Wife. *New York: HarperCollins, 2001.*

—Jennifer Mooney

CHAPTER I

1. *In the old New York of the 'thirties:* In subsequent editions, *'thirties* has become *'fifties.* In 1924, Appleton compiled four of Wharton's novellas—all previously serialized—in a single volume entitled *Old New York: The Old Maid* (serialized in *Red Book,* 1922); *New Year's Day* (*Red Book,* 1923), *False Dawn* (*Ladies' Home Journal,* 1923), and *The Spark* (*Ladies' Home Journal,* 1923). In the tetralogy, the four novellas are for the first time associated with particular periods, as noted by their subtitles: *The Old Maid* becomes a tale of the 'fifties; *New Year's Day,* the 'seventies; *False Dawn,* the 'forties; and *The Spark,* the 'sixties. Interestingly, when Warner Bros. filmed *The Old Maid* in 1939, they changed its date again, this time to the Civil War–era 1860s—presumably to cash in on the popularity of *Gone with the Wind,* notes Sarah Bird Wright. One of the oddest changes in the movie affects the character of Clem Spender, who is no longer an expatriate painter but instead a soldier in the Union Army! For additional information, see Wright's *Edith Wharton A to Z: The Essential Guide to the Life and Work.* To place the story in the 1850s is more logical, since some of the references in it would otherwise be historically inaccurate.

2. *ship chandlers:* people who deal in wares for ships, such as canvas and ropes.

3. *without a sound:* Several textual alterations exist in this paragraph. In subsequent editions, *shipbuilders* becomes *ship-builders.* This is the first of many

terms hyphenated in subsequent editions. *Those well-fed, slow-moving people* loses its comma and becomes *Those well-fed slow-moving people.* Finally, *keyboards* becomes *key-boards.*

4. *not . . . to die for a creed but to live for a bank-account:* The Pilgrims who arrived in Plymouth, Massachusetts, in 1620, and who would later establish the Puritan or Congregational Church, made their journey based on religious convictions, their "creed." They had originally fled England for Holland, which offered greater religious tolerance, but they found the country too liberal, so they opted to sail for the New World. There they hoped not only to practice their religion freely but also to spread the Word. Writing in *Of Plymouth Plantation* (Chapter 4), William Bradford (1590–1657) identifies the Pilgrims' goal as "laying the foundation . . . for the propagating and advancing of the kingdom of Christ in those remote parts of the world."

5. *edulcorated Church of England:* Something that has been "edulcorated" (a term rarely used in modern times) has been purified or freed from its harsh properties. Wharton thus intimates, rather sarcastically, that the form taken by the American version of the Church of England is new and improved. The history of the Church of England in America has two periods: pre- and post–Revolutionary War. In the period before the war, the American version of the Church was—quite obviously—more closely aligned with that of England and was, in fact, under the jurisdiction of the Bishop of London. After the Revolutionary War, Church adherents sought to create their own Episcopal Church of the United States of America, but initially they ran into a major obstacle: their own priests could not be made bishops by their English counterparts because they would have had to swear an Oath of Allegiance to the Crown—which they clearly could not do. The Rev. Samuel Seabury, the first American bishop, was consecrated by Scottish bishops, but eventually an Act of Parliament made it possible for English bishops to confer episcopates upon men who were not British subjects.

6. *coarser allusions in the Marriage Service . . . the comminatory passages in the Athanasian Creed:* Although the Reformation effectively desacralized marriage, during the Renaissance the Anglican Church "made every effort to emphasize its worth and dignity," according to Marilyn Yalom in *A History of the Wife.* One of the ways it did so was to reverse the negative view of marital sexual relations predominant during the medieval period and to instead emphasize the joys of "nuptial love," which involved the joining of man and woman in "heart, body, and mind." Today, some versions of the marriage service are even more blatant, as is the Common Worship Service of the Church of England, which refers to the "delight and tenderness of sexual union." The Athanasian Creed threatens that those who do not adhere to the Catholic faith shall "perish everlastingly" and "cannot be saved." These are perhaps the comminatory passages to which Wharton refers.

7. *sea-plants:* subsequently *seaplants.*

8. *fly kites:* Given the context, the most likely explanation for this term is to experiment with something or speculate financially.

9. *"those damned springs":* If it were not for the fact that the location of said springs is "down south," the most logical candidate for this reference would be Saratoga Springs, which is located in New York State. However, given the geographical reference, Old John Frederick Ralston is most likely referring to the resort of White Sulphur Springs, Virginia (now West Virginia). In the nineteenth century, visits to mineral and natural springs were extremely popular. Balneotherapy, the use of natural and mineral water to improve the health and prevent disease, was current, and beyond that, such spas boasted additional benefits: they were great social gathering spots. In subsequent editions, *damned springs* becomes *d——d Springs.*

10. *"The way we've always done it":* In this paragraph, *than any of our own kind* becomes *or any of our own kind,* while *with their young fellows* becomes *after their young fellows.*

11. *revered Hamilton and served Jefferson:* Essentially, the cautious New York gentlemen of whom Wharton writes followed the more democratic tenets of Thomas Jefferson (1743–1826) even while they longed in their hearts for an aristocracy, which was more along the lines of Alexander Hamilton's (1755–1804) philosophy. In short, while Jefferson believed in the common man, supported the middle and lower classes, and conceived of a government more democratic in orientation, Hamilton thought the wealthy should run society, supported the upper classes, and considered the British aristocracy to be a fine model for American government.

12. *longed to lay out New York like Washington, and who laid in out instead like a grid-iron, lest they should be thought "undemocratic":* The design for Washington, D.C., involved grand avenues radiating from the houses of Congress and the President, with open areas at intersections where statues could be erected and ceremonial spaces could be established. This design was established in 1791, by Major Pierre-Charles L'Enfant (1754–1825), who was clearly French.

13. *substance and color:* In this paragraph, *Shopkeepers* becomes *Shop-keepers* and the comma is omitted from *where, through lack of use* so that it becomes *where through lack of use.* Finally, *color* becomes *colour* (this change occurs throughout).

14. *the Cause:* the fight for American independence from England.

15. *of a ruling class:* In this paragraph, *present generation* becomes *fourth generation; honor* becomes *honour* (the first of many words to adopt a British spelling); and *They themselves had done little* becomes *The Ralstons had done little.*

16. *all the old-established charities:* According to Marvin Olansky, nineteenth-century New York was the "most charitable city in the world." Among the over one thousand charitable organizations which sprang up during the period were the Society for the Relief of Poor Widows with Small Chil-

dren (1797), the New York Society for the Prevention of Pauperism (1816), the Children's Aid Society of New York (1853), and the Society for the Relief and Aid of Poor Women. Perhaps one of the most well-known was the New York Society for the Prevention of Cruelty to Children, but it was not established in 1875. See Olansky, "Beyond the Stingy Welfare State: What We Can Learn from the Compassion of the 19th Century," *Policy Review* 54 (Fall 1990).

17. *the American sculptors in Rome whose reputation was already made:* During the nineteenth century, American sculptors flocked to Italy, where they could find readily available fine-grade marble, as well as craftsmen who could capably and faithfully copy their work. Among the women who traveled there for artistic reasons were Harriet Hosmer (1830–1908), Emma Stebbins (1815–82), and Edmonia Lewis (ca. 1845–1911), who was of African-American and Native American heritage. They joined men like Horatio Greenough (1805–52), who was the first to study in Italy and who actually settled in Florence; Thomas Crawford (1814–57), and Shobal Clevenger (1812–43). Wharton most likely has in mind, though, the sculptor Hiram Powers (1805–73), who gained international fame for his neoclassical busts of Washington and Andrew Jackson. This phrase also contains a textual alteration: in later editions, *was already made* becomes *was already established.*

18. *three-per-cent investment:* later, *three per cent.*

19. *The marriage . . . had been solemnized, as was then the custom, in the drawing-room of the bride's country home:* Until the late medieval period, marriage services were most often conducted in the home of the bride. Those conducted "at church" literally were conducted *at* rather than *in:* bride, groom, and priest gathered either at the church entrance or on a side porch. However, in 1563, the Council of Trent decreed that all marriages must take place inside a church—a demand most probably based on the Catholic Church's recognition of marriage as a sacrament. In the Episcopal Church, to which the families in Wharton's novella would have belonged, the location of the ceremony would more likely have been bound to tradition, fashion, or, as Wharton puts it, "custom." For additional information on marriages, see Yalom, *A History of the Wife.*

20. *hammer-cloth:* the cloth covering the driver's seat in a coach.

21. *new houses in Gramercy Park:* In the 1840s and 1850s, brick mansions and brownstones or town houses began to crop up in Gramercy Park, which is located between East 18th and East 21st streets, between Park and Third avenues. The house lots, which faced the private park, were among the most prestigious, exclusive places to live in New York during the nineteenth century. Interestingly, only a few years earlier, this location had been a swamp. It was purchased and reclaimed by Sam Ruggles in 1831. In 1845, there were only twelve houses located on the square. Also, from this sentence, in subsequent editions, a comma has been omitted: *shaded streets, to one of the new houses* becomes *shaded streets to one of the new houses.*

22. *pin-money:* money to be used for incidental household expenses, perhaps so-called because it could and often was literally pinned inside one's clothing to be within ready reach.

23. *her kindly Jim:* In this paragraph, *she sat one day* becomes *she sat one afternoon; that tremor in her of the muted keyboard* becomes *that tremor of the muted key-board;* the colon becomes a semicolon after *fleeting;* and *housekeeping* becomes *house-keeping.*

24. *low-cut Cluny collar:* The brooch of St. Peter's most likely depicts, in minimosaic, St. Peter's Square in Rome. This design did exist in the nineteenth century. Delia's collar is made of lace, named for the town in eastern France where its style originated. Cluny lace collars, which were removable, were popular adornments to Victorian dresses and blouses.

25. *Cashmere scarf:* Delia's scarf is made of the fine, soft wool from the undercoat of the cashmere goat, native to the Himalayas.

26. *as quick as a girl's:* In this paragraph, *matron* subsequently becomes *wife, gray* becomes *grey* (the British spelling occurs elsewhere in the later editions, so no further reference will be made to it), and the comma is omitted after *in the void.* Also, after this paragraph, the section break that occurs is omitted from subsequent editions.

27. *Mrs. Ralston:* subsequently, *Mrs. Jim Ralston.*

28. *cabriolet:* In this case, a bonnet shaped like the vehicle, which is a two-wheeled chaise with a large hood and an ample apron.

29. *marabou:* Delia's bonnet is decorated with the downy feathers of the marabou, a stork-like bird. Subsequently spelled *marabout.*

30. *St. Mark's-in-the-Bouwerie:* Episcopal Church of the period, consecrated in 1799 and located on the corner of Second Avenue and 10th Street. Now known as *St. Mark's in the Bowery.*

31. *Waverley Place:* In addition to Gramercy Park, Waverley Place in what is now Greenwich Village also served as the home of nineteenth-century New York aristocrats. Named after the title character in Sir Walter Scott's (1771–1832) novel *Waverley* (1814), the neighborhood once boasted among its residents Edna St. Vincent Millay (1892–1950) and the grandmother of Henry James (1843–1916). From her home, which was located at what was then Washington Square North and which he visited often, James gained inspiration for his own *Washington Square* (1880).

32. *blushfully:* subsequently, *blushingly.*

33. *scorching the brow of innocence:* This paragraph beautifully depicts how sexuality was approached during the period. Several textual alterations occur in this paragraph: *startled, unprepared surrender* becomes *startled puzzled surrender; accorded a rosy cheek* becomes *yielded a rosy cheek; double bed* becomes *double-bed;* and *the* is added before the two phrases *dreamless double slumbers* and *early-morning discussions.*

34. *as pretty as hers:* The section break that occurs after this paragraph is subsequently omitted.

35. *counterpane:* a coverlet or bedspread.
36. *Colored lithographs of the "Four Seasons" by Léopold Robert:* Louis-Léopold Robert (1794–1835) intended to create four great paintings to represent not just the four seasons but also the four ethnic regions of Italy. *Return from the Fete of the Madonna dell'Arco* depicts the Neopolitans in springtime, while other entries include *Summer Reapers Arriving in the Pontine Marshes* and *Fishers of the Adriatic,* which provides a glimpse of Venice in winter. Depressed due to an unrequited love, Robert did not complete his plan for autumn, which would have depicted Florence's vineyards. Robert committed suicide in 1835.
37. *daguerreotypes:* An early photographic technique invented in roughly 1835 by Louis-Jacques-Mandé Daguerre (1789–1851), the daguerreotype used metal plates that were light sensitive and coated with silver to capture images.
38. *ormolu clock:* This clock would have been gold in color but not in substance: *ormolu* was, in fact, an alloy of copper and tin or zinc that resembled the more precious metal.
39. *Mrs. Manson Mingott:* Wharton has created a complete universe of New York characters, some of whom appear in both *The Age of Innocence* (1920) and *The Old Maid.* For example, Mrs. Manson Mingott figures prominently in *The Age of Innocence,* as the grandmother of May and Ellen Welland. In *The Old Maid,* she becomes Delia's aunt. Once a defiant young woman who broke social rules, Mrs. Mingott in her older years becomes the matriarch of New York society. Other names that crop up in the two works are the van der Luydens (*The Old Maid,* Chapter 1) and Sillerton Jackson (Chapter 6).
40. *Tuileries:* a royal palace on the River Seine, the construction of which was begun under Catherine de Medici in 1564. Finished in the 1600s, this palace served during the French Revolution as a home for Louis XVI and his family; later, Napoleon I also lived there. After the Restoration, the site became the official royal residence. While the edifice was destroyed in 1871, its huge and elaborate gardens remain.
41. *bold shepherd stealing his kiss:* In this paragraph, in subsequent editions, a comma is added after *"valanced" border; the wardrobe* becomes *a wardrobe; Colored lithographs* becomes *Coloured lithographs; deeply recessed* becomes *deeply-recessed; timepiece* becomes *time-piece; intrusted by her* becomes *entrusted by Mrs. Mingott; or had consented* becomes *or if he had consented;* and the placement of the semicolon and closing quotation after *Palais Royal* becomes inverted.
42. *lung-fever:* While *lung-fever* refers most generally to pneumonia, the fact that Charlotte's weak lungs seem to have been inherited from her father might suggest that the illness was actually a form of consumption, which was rampant during the nineteenth century in both America and England and was thought to be genetic.
43. *"up the River":* It is believed that this slang phrase originated with respect to

the location Sing Sing Prison, which is located up the Hudson River from New York City; thus, one of its meanings is *to be imprisoned;* i.e., sent up the river (to Sing Sing). However, it is hardly likely that the Widow Lovell was in prison; rather, it seems that here the phrase takes its alternative meaning: *to live in hardship* or under constraints (in this case, monetary).

44. *her mother's turned garments:* Often, the sleeves and collars—even, depending upon the material, entire portions—of dresses were literally turned inside out and resewn into place when they were handed down.

45. *"opened a ball":* In other words, danced the first dance. If this ball was a cotillion, which is likely, Charlotte's great-aunt would have been one of the debutantes introduced to society during the occasion.

46. *Charlotte Lovell was going to be an old maid:* In this paragraph, the following alterations were made in subsequent editions: *defunct great-aunt* becomes simply *defunct aunt; saw herself gradually banishing* becomes *saw herself banishing; timepiece* becomes *time-piece;* and *"not quite nice."* becomes *not "quite nice."*

47. *tarlatan:* open-weave muslin, a thin fabric that was usually starched stiffly to give it resilience and "body."

48. *made her look as if she painted:* In other words, Chatty's natural blush makes her look as though she is wearing makeup. Recall Hamlet's tirade against Ophelia regarding the same topic: "I have heard of your paintings, well enough. God hath given you one face, and you make yourselves another" (3.1.143-44). Additionally, in the phrase that begins *not to mention,* as is the case with most if not all phrases set off by long dashes in the *Red Book* edition, a comma precedes the first dash and occurs after the last word, prior to the closing dash. In subsequent editions, these commas are removed. Since this change occurs whenever the comma–dash combination is used, it will not be pointed out hereafter.

49. *her hair was well oiled:* Fashionable ladies of the period tamed their unruly curls with pomades like *bandoline,* a preparation for oiling the hair. According to the *Oxford English Dictionary,* bandoline has over time been made from a variety of materials, from quince pulp to a mixture of linseed oil and rosewater.

50. *delicate cheeks, under a wreath of red:* Subsequently, the comma is removed from this phrase.

51. *known to have called her pretty:* The section break that occurs at the end of this paragraph is omitted from later editions.

52. *plain dresses of Quakerish cut:* Quaker fashion was austere and simple; hence, a dress with a "Quakerish cut" would have been high-necked and long-sleeved, usually with voluminous skirts that would have hidden the shape of the body beneath. Generally, the colors of choice were black and gray.

53. *"day-nursery":* literally, a nursery that cared for children during the day, when their mothers were at work. Night nurseries also existed. Chatty's day nursery exemplifies the growing concern of the more well-to-do for the working poor.

54. *poor children of the neighborhood:* In this paragraph, numerous textual alterations occur: the comma is omitted after *When she came back; poor* becomes *indigent; South* becomes *south; contemporaries* becomes *young friends; with an exchange of significant glances* becomes *with significant glances;* the semicolon and quotation mark are transposed after the phrase *"pass off in time"; grandmother* becomes *grand-mother; the old Mercer Street house* becomes *the old lady's Mercer Street house; poor* becomes *destitute;* and *neighborhood* becomes *neighbourhood.* More importantly, in subsequent editions, a paragraph break does not occur here.

55. *the Battery:* Battery Park—so named for the cannons that once protected Castle (or Fort) Clinton, located there—is a green space on the Hudson River. During the nineteenth century, concerts were held at Castle Garden in the Battery, and it served as a recreation or pleasure spot for walkers.

56. *pinned to the baby's cloak:* Subsequently, *intense curiosity in the neighborhood two or three years earlier* becomes *intense curiosity two or three years earlier; veiled lady in handsome clothes* becomes *veiled lady in a handsome cloak; Dr. Lanskell was the chief practitioner of the day, and presumably versed* becomes *Dr. Lanskell, the chief medical practitioner of the day, was presumably versed; but though beset* becomes *but, though beset; hundred-dollar bill* becomes *hundred dollar bill;* and *baby's cloak* becomes *baby's bib.*

57. *pickaninnies:* a phrase believed to be of West Indian origination, used to describe children of African descent.

58. *Grandmamma Lovell's stable:* In this paragraph, the two semicolons in the first sentence are changed to commas subsequently, the comma after *toddle* is removed, *day nursery* becomes *day-nursery, fellow-paupers* becomes *fellow paupers, in marriage and motherhood* becomes simply *in marriage,* and *plebeian waifs* becomes merely *waifs.*

59. *many a reel and Schottisch:* A reel is a fast-paced dance of Scottish origin. A Schottische or Scottische is either a polka-like dance that originated in England in 1848 or, if denominated a Highland or Balmoral Scottische, a lively dance reminiscent of the Highland Fling. Subsequently, *Schottisch* becomes *schottishe.*

60. *the Ralston mothers chorused:* In this paragraph, *Delia playfully sounded* becomes *Delia sounded; no more questions* becomes *no further questions; Now it became evident* becomes *Now it was clear; an old romance, probably* becomes *an old romance between them, probably;* the semicolon and closing quotation mark are transposed after "misunderstanding"; *were about to ring* becomes *preparing to ring;* and the period that closes the paragraph becomes ellipses.

61. *poplin:* a ribbed fabric used in making clothing and furniture; can be as soft as silk or as stiff as wool.

62. *brown cashmere:* subsequently, *grey cashmere.*

63. *crystals glittered:* Subsequently, this sentence reads *Delia, lifting her hands, removed the white bonnet from her dark polished head, and shook it gently to make the crystals glitter.*

64. *tippet:* A shoulder covering usually made—as it is in this case—of fur. Long and generally thin in width, the tippet is draped across the shoulders as with a shawl. Additionally, in this sentence, *dove-colored* has become *dove-coloured* and Chatty's dress is covered not merely with *rows of crimson velvet ribbon* but with *narrow rows* of the same.

65. *hair is darker:* subsequently, *hair certainly is darker.*

66. *fleeting glare:* In this paragraph, the sentence *Charlotte broke out in her deep voice, pushing back one of the pomaded bands that framed her face, and showing a white lock on her temple.* becomes *Charlotte suddenly broke out in her deep voice. She pushed back one of the pommaded bands that framed her face, and showed a white lock on her temple.* The phrase *added harshly* become simply *added,* while *her teeth* becomes *her small white teeth.*

67. *marabou up:* Here, *the white bonnet* becomes merely *the bonnet,* while *marabou up* becomes *marabout-up.*

68. *incoherently summed up:* subsequently, *incoherently cried.*

69. *said Charlotte wearily:* subsequently, *said Charlotte Lovell wearily.*

70. *Axminster carpet:* In Axminster, England, in the 1700s, Thomas Whitty developed a pattern for hand-knotting carpets, subsequently identified as *Axminster weaving.* Such carpets were similar in strength, value, and beauty to Persian carpets; hence, they were quite expensive.

71. *shrinking slippers:* The section break that occurs after this paragraph is subsequently removed.

72. *she cried:* subsequently, *she questioned.*

73. *". . . he would have provided for it before—":* In this paragraph, the ellipsis with four points in the first line becomes a long dash; *Delia cried* becomes *Delia exclaimed; Joe's past—not that* becomes *Joe's past—? Not that;* the comma in *hint, never* becomes a semicolon; the dash after *if there were* is replaced by an ellipsis; and the dash after *that he's been* has been replaced by an ellipsis, as has the dash that ends the paragraph.

74. *'Men will be men;':* Subsequently, the semicolon and closing internal quotation mark are transposed.

75. *sunny, prosperous room:* subsequently, *sunny prosperous room.*

76. *want her to give up?:* Subsequently, the commas that set off the phrase *Delia wondered* are replaced by parentheses, while the comma after *poor Charlotte* has been omitted.

77. *weeping in the cushions:* In this paragraph, *After—after we have children, he's afraid—afraid* becomes *After—after we have children . . . he's afraid . . . afraid;* the series of five ellipsis points after *catch things* becomes four; the dash after *someone* becomes an ellipsis; a comma is added after *a hired person; in a sob* becomes *with a sob;* and *weeping* becomes *prostrate weeping.* Additionally, the section break that occurs after this paragraph is subsequently omitted.

78. *small-pox:* Beginning with such flu-like symptoms as a high fever, headache, and chills, the highly contagious and often fatal disease that is smallpox

soon erupts (pardon the pun) in widespread pustules that leave scars or pockmarks in the flesh. Also, in subsequent editions, *Henry van der Luydens' only child, from small-pox caught at the circus* becomes *Henry van der Luydens' only child, who had caught small-pox at the circus.*

79. *After that warning:* subsequently, *After such a warning as that.*

80. *Brussels lace:* Belgium is renowned for the quality and beauty of its lace; hence, the fact that the lace is from Brussels hints at its expense. In addition, in this sentence, *Her collar of Brussels lace hung in a crumpled wisp on the loose folds of her bodice* becomes *Her collar of Brussels lace had come undone and hung in a wisp on her crumpled bodice.*

81. *In the pale brown of her eyes:* subsequently, *In her pale brown eyes.*

82. *"she seems to have no idea":* subsequently, *she doesn't seem to realize in the least.*

83. *"Your—your?":* subsequently, *Your—your—?*

84. *"You're hurting my wrists, Chatty":* subsequently, *Take care—you're hurting my wrists, Chatty!*

85. *"My own little girl: the one that Jessamine and Cyrus—":* Subsequently, this sentence is broken into two.

86. *her own melted:* In this paragraph, *such things should not have been spoken* becomes *such things, even if they had to be said, should not have been spoken; folds* becomes *organ-like folds;* and *crumpled* become *tumbled.*

87. *"Oh, poor Chatty—poor Chatty!":* subsequently, *Oh, poor Chatty—my poor Chatty!*

Chapter II

1. *certainly have agreed with him:* In this paragraph, *"hundred-dollar baby"* loses its hyphen; *in her own house, from the lips of the victim!* becomes *in her own house, and from the lips of the victim!; in the South, then?* becomes *in the south, then—?; from such speculations, too, her mind recoiled* loses its commas; and *bringing home contagion* becomes *bringing contagion into their home.*

2. *her children as his:* The beginning of this sentence is changed to *The thing was hard to imagine; yet in a flash of mental readjustment, Delia saw herself as Clem's wife, she saw her children as his, she . . .*

3. *Pharisee:* Here, simply a hypocritical person. The term originally referred to a member of the Jewish sect that strictly observed Mosaic law.

4. *"I mean, about yourself—this thing—this—":* Here, all dashes are replaced with ellipses.

5. *"That's over. . . . Now it's only the child. . . . . ":* The first ellipsis is replaced with a dash, while the second set of five points becomes a set of three.

6. *institution:* subsequently, *Institution.*

7. *"took advantage of you—":* This short paragraph contains several revisions: *"No; I suppose not. But you speak as if . . . as if . . . the person who took advantage of you . . ."*

8. *"one day before he said good-by—":* In this paragraph, all dashes are subsequently changed to ellipses, *Mother* is lower-cased, and *good-by* becomes *goodbye* (the last, a change that takes place consistently thereafter).

9. *"To leave the country—knowing?":* subsequently, *"He left the country—knowing?"*

10. *"for a few weeks—":* The dash is subsequently replaced by an ellipsis. Also, at the end of this paragraph, the section break that appears here is subsequently omitted.

11. *Delia stared:* subsequently, *Blindly Delia stared.*

12. *she suddenly asked in a low tone:* subsequently, *she asked at length in a low tone.*

13. *Charlotte broke off irritably:* In subsequent editions, *irritably* is omitted.

14. *wont:* Although *wont* is occasionally presented as *won't* in the *Red Book* edition, it is generally spelled this way. Subsequently, becomes *won't.*

15. *"It's for my baby—my baby—":* Subsequently, the dashes are changed to ellipses.

16. *throttling hand at her throat:* In subsequent editions, the comma is omitted from the phrase *harsh, dry voice; heartbeats* becomes *heart-beats;* and *that they felt like a throttling hand at her throat* becomes *they seemed to send up throttling hands to her throat.*

17. *"clock for your wedding—":* In this paragraph, in subsequent editions, all dashes become ellipses, while the series of five ellipsis points after the phrase *he was sailing* becomes a series of three.

18. *revelations of dishonor?:* The section break that occurs here is missing from subsequent editions.

19. *"I can't give up my baby":* In this paragraph, in subsequent editions, *Charlotte* becomes *Charlotte Lovell,* all dashes become ellipses, and *that* has been added to the last sentence so that it ends *you must see that I can't give up my baby.*

20. *growin horror:* This obvious typesetting error has been corrected in subsequent editions.

21. *her heart:* Subsequently, the following changes occur in this paragraph: *her lips* becomes *her parched lips; Through them* becomes *Through the tears; half guessed* becomes hyphenated, and *her heart* becomes *her own heart.*

22. *plague-houses they called asylums:* During the nineteenth century, a number of children's hospitals or asylums were organized in New York, including the Asylum for the Relief of Half-Orphan and Destitute Children, the Children's Orphanage, the New York House of Refuge, the Orphan Asylum Society (1806), and the New York Foundling Hospital (1869). In an era where sanitary conditions and medical practices were not completely modernized, such places—particularly if crowded—could serve indeed as "plague-houses" for any infectious disease. These refuges were struck by smallpox and other traditionally virulent diseases, but they also played host to such illnesses as pellagra, a diet-based disease common among those who lived in poor, overcrowded conditions.

23. *turned back to her cousin:* In this paragraph, these changes occur: a comma is inserted after the first word in *But in any case;* the comma is removed from the phrase *charity, in a negro hovel; asylums* is capitalized.

24. *Granny Lovell:* In this paragraph, the two series of five ellipsis points are re-

duced in number to three, while the final period has been replaced with an ellipsis.

25. *plain bonnet and heavy veil:* Subsequently, the following changes were made in this paragraph: a period is inserted after the phrase that ends *you would go home,* although the dash remains; the dash after *stay here* becomes a colon, and the comma is omitted after *wardrobe.*

26. *Feverishly she had unfolded:* becomes *Feverishly, Delia unfolded.*

27. *muff:* A staple of nineteenth-century outerwear, a muff is cylindrical in shape, carried at waist-level (often, strings secure it around the neck), and usually made of fur or other warm material, with openings on either end into which the hands are inserted for warmth.

28. *"You'll wait?" Delia insisted:* becomes more specifically a command: *"You'll wait," Delia insisted.*

29. *"Yes; I'll wait":* becomes *"Yes: I'll wait."*

CHAPTER III

1. *Highland cap and broadcloth spencer:* The Highland cap worn by Delia's son is most likely a tam-o'-shanter. A spencer is a short, double-breasted coat popular among men and boys during the period. A spencer was also designed for women. To the paragraph in which these phrases occur, the following changes have been made: the comma is omitted after *park-rails; Park-dwellers* becomes *square-dwellers;* and *broadcloth* becomes hyphenated.

2. *"mews":* a small street in which smaller apartments or dwellings are located.

3. *deal table:* a table made of pine or fir.

4. *Miss Charlotte:* To this paragraph, subsequent editions make these changes: the comma is omitted from *sturdy, old-fashioned,* and the words *honeymoon* and *whitewashed* become hyphenated. Additionally, the section break that occurs after this paragraph is omitted.

5. *alpaca:* the fine, fleecy wool of the alpaca, an animal that resembles a llama.

6. *fingered her watch-chain:* In this paragraph, several changes occur: *playing, and huddled* becomes *playing and, huddled;* the comma is omitted from *rich, rustling; They* becomes *Those buttons;* and *Delia stooped* becomes *Delia stopped.*

7. *"The floor aint none too clean":* becomes *"The floor here ain't none too clean."*

8. *The little creature on her knee was made of different stuff:* Traditionally, one is able to tell that a kidnapped, disguised, or orphaned child is royal or a member of the elite class by what Northrop Frye calls a "talisman of recognition" (in this case, Tina's curls growing in points, like those of her father). The motif of the orphan child recurs throughout literature. See Frye, *The Secular Scripture: A Study of the Structure of Romance.*

9. *finger the chain in silence:* In this short paragraph, *Delia unfastened it* becomes *Delia unfastened the gold chain,* while *finger the chain in silence* becomes *finger the links in silence.*

10. *"those blacks—":* becomes *those blacks . . .*

11. *"There, there now!"*: In this paragraph, *Miss Chatty aint been in yet, and she's kinder lonesome* becomes *Miss Chatty ain't been in today, and the little thing's kinder lonesome,* while the ellipsis points have been reduced in number in the first two cases from five to three. Finally, the exclamation point which ends the paragraph has been replaced by a series of three ellipsis points.

12. *stableyard:* becomes *stable-yard.*

13. *"I mean to keep her":* In this paragraph, the following changes occur: the colon after *Listen* becomes a period, and *sha'n't* becomes *shan't*. This last change is consistent throughout.

14. *onto her poplin skirt:* The semicolon after *to speak* becomes a comma, while a comma has been added after *to her mouth.*

15. *"Charlotte—Charlotte!":* The exclamation point becomes a simple comma.

16. *vinaigrette . . . acrid aromatic scent:* A vinaigrette is a small, usually rectangular box that, with the addition of a chain, could be worn around the neck or carried within easy reach in a pocket. Inside rests a tiny piece of sponge soaked with an aromatic vinegar (sometimes tempered with lavendar), which serves as an alternative to smelling salts.

17. *"Oh!" Charlotte moaned:* The exclamation point becomes a simple comma.

18. *"Only trust me":* In this paragraph, the five ellipsis points after *my own way* turn into three, while the final period is replaced by a series of three ellipsis points.

19. *"The tears—don't dry them, Delia. I like to feel them.":* becomes *"The tears . . . don't dry them, Delia. . . . like to feel them . . ."* Also the section break that occurs after this line of dialogue is subsequently omitted.

20. *There was a knock:* In this paragraph, subsequent editions show these changes: *The two cousins leaned against each other* becomes *The two cousins continued to lean against each other,* the semicolon after *declined and darkened* becomes a comma, and *Axminster carpet* becomes merely *Axminster.*

21. *Mother:* becomes lowercased.

Chapter IV

1. *did not do likewise:* In this paragraph, the semicolon after *reluctantly* becomes a comma, the comma is omitted after *new one,* and *did not do likewise* becomes *did not immediately do likewise.*

2. *two days' resistance:* Subsequent editions omit the comma after *resistance.*

3. *Nottingham lace curtains:* Nottingham, England, has long been famous for its lace. In fact, the town has an entire Lace Market.

4. *whatnots:* Although today the term "whatnot" is used almost exclusively as a synonym for "knick-knack," in this case it refers to the light shelves on which knick-knacks were placed.

5. *tropical shells, feldspar vases . . . the newer knick-knacks:* The mineral feldspar consists of silicates of aluminum with either potassium, sodium, calcium, or barium. Porphyry is a fine-grained rock that contains large crystals, like feldspar. Serpentine, often used for building, is a green, brown, or spotted

mineral. The miniature bust of Clytie is perhaps a reference to the masterwork of American sculptor William Henry Rinehart (1825–74). While the original was done in marble, this version is done in fine French porcelain or *biscuit de Sevres*. Chelsea ware is china made during the eighteenth century in Chelsea, London.

6. *Cole's "Voyage of Life," . . . Eglinton's tournament:* Hudson River landscape painter Thomas Cole (1801–48) actually produced two different versions of the series of four paintings entitled *The Voyage of Life*, but both explore the transition from childhood to old age. The series, from 1842, depicts childhood, youth, manhood, and old age. Joseph Mallord William Turner (1775–1851) produced a series of engravings that was collectively known as *The Rivers of France* (1835). The longest and most serious poem produced by the American poet and satirist Joseph Rodman Drake (1795–1820) was *Culprit Fay* (1835). English doctor, minister, and writer George Crabbe (1754–1832) is known for several collections of tales, particularly *Tales in Verse* (1812) and *Tales of the Hall* (1819). In 1839, after a year of planning, Archibald William Montgomerie, the 13th Earl of Eglinton, conducted a medieval tournament at his family estate in Ayrshire, in Scotland. The event attracted thousands of visitors from across Great Britain, Europe, and America. In this long paragraph, numerous changes are made in subsequent editions: *parlor* becomes *parlour; striped silk* becomes *striped moire; favorite* becomes *favourite; center-table* becomes *centre-table;* the comma is omitted after *damasks; whatnots* becomes *what-nots; feldspar* becomes *feldspar; a small bust of Clytie in* biscuit de Sèvres becomes *a bust of Clytie in chalk-white* biscuit de Sevres; *knick-knacks* becomes *ornaments; Great-grandmamma* becomes lowercased; and *On the damask wall-paper* becomes *On the walls.* (Note: the British spellings are hereafter consistent in later editions.) The collection of art also changes: after *Cole's "Voyage of Life,"* is added *and between the windows stood the life-size statue of "A Captive Maiden" executed for Jim Ralston's father by the celebrated Harriet Hosmer, immortalized in Hawthorne's novel of the Marble Faun.* What rests on the table becomes a separate sentence, and the quotation marks around the titles of the artworks or books are subsequently omitted.

7. *hard-coal fire:* There are essentially two types of coal: *bituminous,* or soft coal, which is generally found in the southern and western states, and *anthracite,* or hard coal, which is found in Pennsylvania. New York's coal supplies would most likely have come from neighboring Pennsylvania.

8. *citron-wood table:* A citron is an Asian tree that bears fruit similar to lemons.

9. *yet turn about as she would:* A comma is added after *yet.*

10. *discover:* becomes *find.*

11. *of the Ralstons collectively:* In this paragraph, *latchkey* becomes *latch-key; or two tall hats* becomes *or of two tall hats;* the dash after *came in* becomes a colon; the colon after *were alike* becomes a semicolon.

12. *Jim with a toothache:* In this paragraph, a comma is added between *yet* and *al-*

lowing: the comma is omitted from *tall, athletic,* as well as from *short, sanguine; the candid blue eyes* becomes *candid blue eyes;* the comma is omitted from *sweet, selfish;* and *toothache* becomes *tooth-ache.*

13. *potluck:* becomes *pot-luck.*

14. *home unannounced:* Subsequently, *unannounced* is omitted.

15. *"Wait till you're married, Joseph Ralston!":* The exclamation point becomes a dash.

16. *Oyster soup . . . corn fritters:* On the menu, *broiled shad* becomes *broiled bass,* while *corn fritters* becomes *apple fritters.*

17. *Rumor:* adopts the British spelling: *rumour.*

18. *Madeira:* an enriched dessert wine originating from the island of Madeira.

19. *counseled:* becomes *counselled.*

20. *wool-work:* needlework, the preferred recreation of the nineteenth-century woman, both in America and in England. Delia's choice of work is perhaps ironic, since she deviates quite obviously from the stereotypical *angel in the house* popular during the period. References to needlework in general often served as the avenue by which nineteenth-century women writers critiqued the era's conception of proper femininity. In *Aurora Leigh,* for example, Elizabeth Barrett Browning (1806–61) writes: "We sew, sew, prick our fingers, dull our sight, / Producing what? A pair of slippers, sir, / To put on when you're weary—or a stool / To stumble over and vex you."

21. *sword of Damocles:* As the story goes, Damocles was a famous flatterer in the court of Dionysius II in Sicily during the fourth century B.C. He loved to compliment Dionysius on his power and wealth, but the ruler grew tired of his behavior and decided to teach him a lesson. He invited Damocles to a great feast, where food and drink were abundant. Damocles was placed on the best cushion in the house, but when he looked up, he discovered a sword hanging over his head, affixed to the ceiling not by a rope but by the thinnest of hairs. Since then, the phrase "sword of Damocles" has come to represent personal danger.

22. *marry him:* In this paragraph, *his exposition* becomes *his embarassed exposition,* the colon after *canvas* becomes a semicolon, and the period after *marry him* becomes an ellipsis.

23. *bowed to the ineluctable:* In this paragraph, *honor* adopts the British spelling, a comma is added between *him seemed,* and *dishonorable* adopts the British spelling.

24. *But yet it must not be:* In this paragraph, the colon after the initial *No* becomes a semicolon, the comma in *on her, she remembered* is omitted, and the comma after *cry* becomes a colon. Also, the section break that occurs here is subsequently omitted.

25. *he flung back at it:* In this paragraph, the comma is omitted after *allowance; Joe was droning on* becomes enclosed in parentheses; *special sum for her poor children* becomes *special sum set apart for her poor children;* the comma after *children* becomes a dash, the dash after *pin-money* becomes a semi-

colon; *the children* becomes *these children;* the dashes around *until* become ellipses, *till nearer duties claim her. . . . . Why, I'm more than ready—if you'll tell her so* becomes *till nearer duties claim her, why, I'm more than ready . . . if you'll tell her so.*

26. *"I should never give up those children":* *should* becomes *could.*

27. *unpunished!:* The exclamation point becomes a dash.

28. *admonished:* becomes *admonished him.*

29. *"Well, whatever—in reason—":* becomes *"Well, that is to say, whatever—in reason—."*

30. *"What more—":* A question mark is added after the dash.

31. *"Nothing more—except this":* The dash becomes a colon.

32. *"pull yourself together, old boy":* becomes *"buck up, old boy."*

33. *"She'll tell you tomorrow":* becomes *"She'll tell you herself tomorrow."*

34. *"Delia's right—":* The dash becomes a semicolon.

35. *easy, good-natured:* The comma is subsequently omitted.

36. *boyish tears:* becomes *a boyish tear.*

37. *Jim admonished him:* becomes *Jim insisted.*

38. *sent abroad to be cured by balmy Italy:* Just as today individuals with "breathing" illnesses such as tuberculosis and asthma are advised to seek drier, warmer climates, in the nineteenth century the same advice was given, with the usual destinations being Italy and the French Riviera. In 1840, British physician George Boddington became one of the first in the medical profession to support climate change as a way of alleviating the effects of tuberculosis. Among those who sought out the warmer climate of Italy to help with their illnesses were John Keats and Lord Chesterfield's wife.

39. *"how am I to tell Charlotte?":* In this paragraph, the comma after *cemetery* becomes a colon; *graveyards* becomes hyphenated; *and the vision* becomes merely *the vision.*

40. *abruptly:* becomes *abruptly from the threshold.*

41. *one of compassion:* In this paragraph, the period after *sends for you* becomes a dash, the sentence that begins *And she winced* becomes a continuation of the previous clause, and the period after *compassion* becomes an ellipsis.

42. *drew away:* becomes *drew apart.*

43. *"What should you have done, Jim":* Before this line of dialogue is subsequently added the sentence *She held him at arms' length.*

44. *"Come!" His strong arm entreated her:* The exclamation point becomes a comma, and the sentence continues: *"Come," his strong arm entreated her.*

45. *grave in sympathy:* becomes *grave, in instant sympathy.*

46. *relieved his pain:* In this paragraph, *Lucky, after all, she has those paupers* becomes *Lucky, now, after all, that she has those paupers;* the comma is omitted after *somebody else's;* and *that the remedy* becomes *the thought of the remedy.*

47. *"Between us, darling,"—and now she let him have her hands,—:* becomes *"Between us, darling—" and now she let him have her hands—*

48. *"Unless she's sent to Italy?":* becomes *"Unless indeed she's sent to Italy?"*

49. *"sum from my pin-money—"*: In this paragraph, *And besides* becomes *And, besides,* and the final dash is replaced by an ellipsis.
50. *Their hands glowed together:* Glowed becomes *flowed.* In this same paragraph, the colon after *eyes* is replaced by a semicolon.
51. *"Not a penny from your pin-money!"*: The end of this sentence is altered: *"Not a penny from your pin-money—never!"*
52. *"When I think of our own upstairs!"*: A comma is added after *own.*

CHAPTER V

1. *cousin's step on the threshold:* becomes simply *cousin's step.*
2. *"I want to see your face, Chatty—unless"*: The dash becomes a colon.
3. *before she sailed for Italy!:* In this paragraph, *window-curtains* becomes *window curtains; let a ray of light into the room* becomes *let in a ray of light; head livid* is separated by a comma; *brick-red* becomes *brick-rose; Just so poor Cousin So-and-so* becomes *Just so, she remembered, poor cousin So-and-so.*
4. *approached:* changes to *drew near.*
5. *own—but now?:* becomes *her own. But now?*
6. *"you'd like best"*: In this paragraph, the semicolon after *dear* becomes a colon, and the period at the end of the sentence is replaced by an ellipsis.
7. *rose sharply:* changes to *sat up sharply.*
8. *"I had hoped such follies!"*: In this paragraph, the dash after *no* is replaced by a colon. Additionally, the two sentences here become a single sentence connected by a dash.
9. *"No, dear—but that you must not marry Joe"*: The dash becomes a semicolon.
10. *"Well, that's done: you shall always be together"*: The colon becomes a semicolon.
11. *"He considers that"*: changed to *He has been given to understand that.* Also, later in this paragraph, the comma is omitted after *For heaven's sake.*
12. *bronze kid:* Chatty's shoes are made of goatskin. Also, several changes occur in this paragraph: *closed eyes* becomes *closed eyes and narrowed lips;* the sentence *Almost like a corpse she lay there* is added immediately thereafter, and the final period of the paragraph becomes an ellipsis.
13. *As the tears reached Chatty's lips, she spoke:* In this paragraph, *her eyes on the closed face* becomes *her eyes on her cousin's closed face; two tears that forced a way* becomes *a tear that forced a way; Chatty's lips* becomes *the narrowed lips.*
14. *"Just she and I?"*: becomes *"Just she and I together?"*
15. *"In a little house."*: The period becomes an ellipsis.
16. *diamond cluster ring:* In this paragraph, *slipped a hand under her pillow* becomes *sent a hand groping under the pillow* and *diamond cluster ring* becomes simply *diamond ring.*
17. *She said:* becomes *she said simply.*

CHAPTER VI

1. *engagement with Joe Ralston:* In this paragraph, several changes occur: *Everyone agreed afterward that you could always have told* becomes *You could always*

have told, every one agreed afterward; the comma is omitted after *before her ill-ness,* as well as from in front of *in spite of her fiery hair; for breaking her* becomes *for her breaking her.*

2. *if Charlotte died:* In this paragraph, subsequent changes include: the clause *the previous experiment in Georgia had been unsuccessful* is inserted after the one that ends *send her to Italy; farmhouse* becomes *farm-house;* the comma is omitted after *property; when the Doctor decided* becomes *when it was decided; Doctor* becomes lowercased; *poor children* becomes *pauper children;* and the semicolon after *their little farmhouse* becomes a comma. The most interesting alteration, however, is the correction of an error. In this edition, Charlotte's intended is identified as *Jim* Ralston rather than *Joe.* The error is corrected in subsequent editions.

3. *share her task:* In this paragraph, changes include: *Charlotte did not die till long afterward* becomes simply *Charlotte did not die;* the comma is omitted after *took place; housewife* becomes *house-wife;* a comma is added between *that* and *when;* and *heartbroken* becomes *heart-broken.* In this edition, the paragraph ends with the words *share her task,* but in subsequent editions, the paragraph continues.

4. *a whole asylumful to choose from:* In this paragraph, the following changes occur: a comma is deleted after *When she took Charlotte;* the dash after *too* becomes a colon; *a little dark-haired girl* becomes *a dark-haired child;* a comma is omitted between *odd* and *incisive; who have lived too much alone* becomes *who have lived too much with their elders; But by a natural instinct of imitation* becomes *But, impelled by an instinct of imitation; no one thought it necessary to correct* becomes *no one took the trouble to correct;* the final clause—here set off by a dash—becomes enclosed in parentheses, and *asylumful* becomes *asylumfull.*

5. *she would have been pronounced extremely stylish:* This paragraph includes three changes: the comma is omitted after the closing parenthesis; *pronounced himself immensely struck with Tina's charms* becomes *was immensely struck by Tina's charms; elegances* becomes capitalized.

6. *deprecated beamingly:* A comma is subsequently inserted between these words.

7. *bandoline: See ch. 1, note 49, p. 87.*

8. *and turning her mocking eyes:* Subsequently, a comma is inserted after *and.*

9. *"and it hurts her":* In this paragraph, *as you did just now, dear* becomes *as you did this evening, dear,* while *It's disrespectful!—and it hurts her* becomes *It's disrespectful—you must see that it hurts her.*

10. *five points on the girl's forehead:* The section break that occurs after this paragraph is subsequently omitted.

11. *welcome over Tina's shoulder:* In this paragraph, *a footfall* becomes *a soft foot-fall* and *gave her a glance of welcome* becomes *sent her a glance of welcome.*

12. *this child:* replaced by *Tina.*

13. *dry tone of dismissal:* In this paragraph *she kissed the girl's proffered forehead* becomes *her thin lips touched the girl's proffered forehead,* while the comma is omitted from between *said* and *in.*

14. *her mother's jewels:* In this paragraph, *chair* becomes *seat,* while the comma is omitted from between *thin* and *ringless.*

15. *heard:* changed to *overheard.*

16. *"severe with Tina: on the contrary":* The colon becomes a semicolon.

17. *shuddering loneliness:* In this paragraph, the comma is omitted from between *intuition* and *she,* while *and measured* becomes *and once more measured.*

18. *"I see—I see—":* The dashes are replaced by ellipses.

19. *"A ridiculous, narrow-minded old maid":* The comma is subsequently omitted.

CHAPTER VII

1. *the usual irreproachable New York alliances:* This sentence becomes altered: *both her children had contracted—ever so safely and suitably—the usual irreproachable New York alliances* becomes *both her children had contracted—so safely and suitably—their irreproachable New York alliances.*

2. *with her to the floor above:* In this paragraph, *Delia left* becomes *Delia had left;* the comma after *Gramercy Park* is deleted; *center* becomes *centre;* the semicolon after *age* becomes a comma; and *her old-fashioned bedroom* becomes simply *her bedroom.*

3. *into each other's souls:* In subsequent editions, the comma that follows this phrase is deleted.

4. *small bedroom next to Tina's, left vacant by the bride's departure:* becomes *next to Tina's that had been left vacant by the bride's departure.*

5. *"her girl friends":* In this paragraph, the comma after *whatever* becomes a semicolon and the comma after *boudoir* is omitted.

6. *Delia's nature to oppose her:* In this paragraph, the comma after *girl* is omitted; *it was as if Charlotte* becomes *it seemed as if Charlotte;* and the comma is omitted from between *mute* and *obstinate.*

7. *imagined herself saying to Clem Spender:* In this paragraph, *were unfamiliar* becomes *were strange or unfamiliar; her own past* becomes *Delia's own past;* and *Clem Spender* becomes *Clement Spender.*

8. *taken down to the room next to Tina's:* In this paragraph, *now it flashed a light* becomes *now the discovery had flashed a light;* the colon after *word* becomes a semicolon; and *Next morning she ordered Charlotte's things taken down to the room next to Tina's* becomes *The next morning she gave the order that Charlotte's things should be taken down to the room next to Tina's.* Also, in subsequent editions, a section break is inserted after this paragraph.

9. *keeping her hold on Tina:* In this paragraph, a comma is inserted after *drawing-room; girls had waylaid her* becomes *girls used to waylay her* (and the comma is omitted); and *It sent a pang through Delia to think* becomes *A pang went through Delia at the thought.*

10. *gas-jet:* Manufactured gas was first used for interior lighting in England in 1792, when William Murdock introduced it into his own cottage. By 1807, the first gas streetlights had been installed in London. In the United States, the first gas-powered streetlights were put to use in Baltimore in 1816. Another type of gas—natural—was invented in Fredonia, New York, in 1821. The prevalence of gas as a source for illumination during the nineteenth century gave the period the nostalgic name "the Gaslight Era."

11. *her "beauty sleep":* In this paragraph, numerous changes occur: *extinguishing of the gas-jet* becomes *the putting out of the gas-jet; As she stood there* becomes *As she lingered; voices from the doors* becomes *voices from the adjoining doors; But none came to her, nor was there* becomes *But none came, nor was there;* the comma is omitted from between *hard* and *methodical; good night to her daughter on reaching her room* becomes *goodnight to her daughter;* and *it was not unlikely, Delia reflected, that she had asked to have the room next to her daughter's simply because she wished the girl not to miss her "beauty sleep"* becomes *she might have asked for the room next to her daughter's simply because she did not want the girl to miss her "beauty sleep."*

12. *the gentlest touch:* In this paragraph, the comma after *actions* is omitted; *she attributed to Charlotte* becomes *she found herself attributing to Charlotte; denying poor Charlotte* becomes *envying poor Charlotte; any too open show* becomes *any show;* and the final period becomes an ellipsis.

13. *Delia held out her arms:* In this paragraph, *a faint knock on her door* becomes *a light knock; On the threshold stood Tina in a dressing-gown* becomes *She opened the door, and there stood Tina, in a dressing gown;* and *heartbeat* becomes *heart-beat.* In addition, the last sentence in this paragraph—*With a happy heartbeat Delia held out her arms*—in later editions becomes a new paragraph.

14. *"she's next to you":* In this paragraph, *Delia kissed her lifted forehead* becomes *Delia pressed a long kiss on her lifted forehead* and *But run off now* becomes simply *Run off now.*

15. *as noiselessly as she had come:* In this paragraph, all semicolons are replaced by commas.

Chapter VIII

1. *the Evening Post:* The *New York Evening Post,* founded in 1801 by William Coleman, at the encouragement of Alexander Hamilton. Additionally, both words are italicized in subsequent editions.

2. *of her daughter's absence:* In this paragraph, *Delia Halsey* becomes *young Mrs. John Junius Halsey;* and *It was their custom, on such occasions, for Charlotte* becomes *Their custom, on such occasions, was for Charlotte.*

3. *To gain time, Mrs. Ralston bent over a dropped stitch:* becomes *To gain time before answering, Mrs. Ralston bent over a stitch.*

4. *"being with Tina—":* The section break that occurs after this paragraph is subsequently omitted.

5. *what if young Delia——?* In this paragraph, *intrust* becomes *entrust*, the colon after *daughter* becomes a semicolon, and *talkative* becomes *conversable*.

6. *do, alone:* becomes *do, all alone.*

7. *"I mean as a husband":* A comma is inserted after *mean.*

8. *"talk things out":* In this paragraph, a comma is added after *assent,* and *talk things out* becomes *talk this thing out.*

9. *"Talk things out? You and I? What things?":* becomes *"Talk this thing out? You and I? What thing?"*

10. *agreeable:* The colon that occurs after this word is changed to a semicolon.

11. *sharply lined:* becomes hyphenated.

12. *"difficulty in deciding.":* In this paragraph, *tastes—artistic—literary; they may even* becomes *tastes . . . artistic . . . literary . . . they may even;* and the final period becomes an ellipsis.

13. *straitened:* becomes *strait.*

14. *about—other decisions":* The dash becomes an ellipsis.

15. *"And you think he's hesitating?":* The section break that occurs here is later deleted.

16. *scene, she:* The comma is subsequently omitted.

17. *he has decided not:* The last word becomes italicized.

18. *abruptly:* The colon after this word becomes a semicolon.

19. *his parents' wishes:* In this paragraph, the commas after *profession* and *suppressed* are omitted.

20. *"hope—we must hope—":* The dashes become ellipses.

21. *his withdrawal:* becomes *Lanning's excuses.*

22. *as a body too hastily concealed!:* becomes *as a corpse too hastily buried!*

23. *"characters. But in any case, surely":* becomes *characters . . . But, in any case, surely.*

24. *"whatever it costs me":* In this paragraph, all dashes are replaced with ellipses.

25. *also—hard as it will be:* The dash becomes an ellipsis.

26. *you are insinuating:* becomes *you're insinuating.*

27. *tambour frame:* Another term for *embroidery hoop.* Also, in this paragraph, the colon following *floor* becomes a semicolon.

28. *"your own child—":* The dash becomes a period.

29. *"She's perfect.":* The period becomes an exclamation point.

30. *Let us say, then, that she:* The commas are omitted.

31. *I've waited—waited:* The dash becomes an ellipsis.

32. *"I'm not ungrateful":* In this paragraph, the comma is omitted from *rapid, monotonous;* and the comma is omitted after *broke.*

33. *"What place has it between you and me?":* The section break that occurs after this paragraph is subsequently deleted.

34. *a creature so radiant could tamely submit:* Could becomes *would.*

35. *Delia's nightly kiss:* In this paragraph, *anyone* becomes *any one; blowing out* becomes *putting out;* and *the cousins lighted their candles* becomes *the two cousins lit their bedroom candles.*

36. *reassurance:* The comma after this word is later omitted.

CHAPTER IX

1. *armchair:* becomes hyphenated.

2. *cloistered nun:* In this paragraph, the comma is omitted after *wheedling* and *gayly* becomes *gaily.*

3. *their doctrine:* becomes *the family doctrine.*

4. *But that day:* becomes *But on that day.*

5. *grand tour:* Often uppercased as the *Grand Tour,* this extended period of traveling through Europe was, during the nineteenth century, considered to be a sort of "finishing school" for upper-class men and, when accompanied by a chaperone, women as well. Also, in this paragraph, *inclosing* becomes *enclosing,* and *Charlotte or Tina* becomes *Charlotte or even for Tina.*

6. *on her way downstairs:* In this paragraph, *Delia Ralston's meditation* becomes *her meditation,* the comma is omitted after *open,* and *passed the threshold* becomes *passed Delia's threshold.*

7. *In that case:* becomes *If that were her object.*

8. *Charlotte had gone downstairs: Downstairs* becomes simply *down.*

9. *stars swam in the moonlight:* In this paragraph, *Delia's room* becomes *Delia's bedroom,* the colon after *darkness* becomes a semicolon, *footstep* becomes *footfall,* the semicolon after *surface* becomes a comma, and *marked* becomes *marred.* Also, the section break that occurs here is later omitted.

10. *three years of mourning:* Mourning customs in the nineteenth century were quite elaborate, particularly for women. In addition to the traditional wearing of black, one was expected to enter a period of mourning for the deceased, the length to be determined by the affiliation. In general, women mourned the longest for a spouse—from one to two or more years, or, in extreme cases, as with Queen Victoria of England, for the rest of one's life. Traditionally, one mourned for a parent for between six months and a single year, but longer periods, as here, were not unknown. Also, in this paragraph, the comma after *cousins* is omitted, and *Square* becomes *square.*

11. *downstairs in the darkness?:* In this paragraph, the comma is omitted after *Before long;* the semicolon after *hoof-beats* becomes a comma; *would mount* becomes *mount.*

12. *neuralgia:* a disease of the nervous system involving spasms or bursts of pain. Also, in this paragraph, a comma is added after the conjunction in the phrase *and wrapped,* and the final period is changed to an ellipsis.

13. *bringing Tina:* In this paragraph, *Hoof-beats sounded in Irving Place* becomes *Hoof-beats, muffled by the snow, sounded in Irving Place; stopped a few doors* becomes *stopped again a few doors;* and *John Juniuses* becomes *John Juniuses'.* Also, the section break that occurs after this paragraph is later omitted.

14. *valse:* waltz. Also, in this paragraph, *Tina* becomes *poor Tina.*

15. *she was talking to:* In this paragraph, *penetrating Delia's shawl* becomes *was finding a way through Delia's shawl,* while *beaver hat* becomes *opera hat.*

16. *treading daisies instead of snow:* In this paragraph, *or her daughter* becomes *or*

else her daughter; the colon after *no* becomes a semicolon; the comma after *sort* is omitted; and *have been treading daisies* becomes *have been falling on daisies.*

17. *Latmian solitude:* a reference to the myth of Endymion, the beautiful youth who spent his life sleeping alone in a cave on Mount Latmos (or Latmus). According to one version of the story, Zeus asked Endymion for his one wish, which turned out to be eternal sleep that would preserve his beauty. In another version, the sleep was a punishment Zeus inflicted on Endymion because he had dared to fall in love with Hera, Zeus's wife. However he ended up asleep, though, Endymion was loved by Selene, goddess of the moon, who visited him nightly in the cave and ultimately bore him fifty daughters.

18. *hard Empire sofas:* in the neoclassical French style, with lean lines and firm padding.

19. *caryatids:* from *"Caryatides,"* maidens of the Greek village of Caryae: support columns carved into the shape of the female form.

20. *young figures in each other's arms:* In this paragraph, the comma is omitted between *exposed* and *compact; possible, literally* becomes *possible—literally; such things to happen* becomes *such encounters to take place;* the period after *overhead* becomes an exclamation point; *blank-faced caryatids* becomes *eyeless marble caryatids;* and *pompous carpet* becomes *faded carpet.* Also, the section break that occurs here is later omitted.

21. *"really ought to say, good morning!":* In this paragraph, the five ellipsis points after *home* become three, *mamma* becomes *Mamma,* the five ellipsis points after *cold* become three, the dash after *Lanning* becomes a semicolon, the period after *so kind* becomes an exclamation point, and *Good night* becomes *Goodnight.*

22. *had reached their rooms:* In this paragraph, the comma after *monologue* is omitted, and *the unlit house-front* becomes *the house-front.*

23. *knelt long by her bedside:* becomes *knelt by her bedside.*

CHAPTER X

1. *a Ralston through and through:* In this paragraph, *seventeen years* becomes *twenty years,* and the colon after *life* becomes a semicolon. Also, in later editions, a section break occurs after this paragraph.

2. *Smyrna rug:* a carpet woven in Smyrna, once one of the richest trading centers in the Levant, in the eastern Mediterranean. Also, in this paragraph, a number of changes occur. *Dr. Lanskell no longer practiced* becomes *For some years now Dr. Lanskell had no longer practised; he went to a few* becomes *he continued to go to;* the conjunction *and* is added after *patients; gave consultations* becomes *to give consultations; his own kingdom* becomes *his former kingdom; lay pope or medical elder* becomes *lay Pope or medical Elder; he had healed* becomes *he had once healed; now returned* becomes *often returned.*

3. *totem-ridden:* The society Wharton writes about is most assuredly ruled by totems: by clans and by customs, both of which are represented in this concept.

4. *Dying Gladiators and Young Augustuses:* perhaps a reference to statues or other works imitative of classical art given to the doctor as gifts. Also, in this paragraph, *Delia sat by his grate* becomes *Delia sat and watched; rows of calf bindings* becomes *rows of medical books in calf bindings;* and *communicated* becomes *given.*

5. *"Delia Lovell":* In this paragraph, *in a genial thump* becomes *with a genial thump* and *Thank God* becomes *Thank goodness.*

6. *Ralston, it:* The comma is later omitted.

7. *gouty bulk:* Gout is a disease caused by an imbalance of uric acid in the body, characterized by painful inflammation of the hands, feet, knees, and other joints. Similar in its effects to arthritis, gout is found almost exclusively in men and was once associated with the upper class, whose diet was more rich and indulgent than that of others. Also, in this paragraph, *chair* becomes *armchair.*

8. *ironic spectacles:* Dr. Lanskell's spectacles are ironic in that while he might need them to improve his vision, he actually "sees" things—situations, society, controversial issues—more clearly than those around him who have perfect 20/20 vision.

9. *"people will say—":* The dash becomes an ellipsis.

10. *"Or else"—:* becomes *"Or else—"*

11. *"He knew?":* becomes *"He knew—?"*

12. *in the baby's interest:* The comma after this phrase is later omitted.

13. *"Oh, Dr. Lanskell!":* The exclamation point later becomes a dash.

14. *at fifty:* becomes *at forty-five.*

15. *"third-and-fourth-generation idea":* This sentence later ends with a dash.

16. *maidservant:* becomes hyphenated.

17. *eyebrows:* becomes hyphenated.

18. *recognize:* becomes *recognize in time.*

19. *brown dining-room:* becomes simply *dining-room.*

20. *it was the accepted attitude:* becomes *it was in those days the accepted state.*

21. *for decisive measures:* In this paragraph, *midday* becomes hyphenated; *resolution was definitely taken* becomes *decision was final; evidently confirmed* becomes *no doubt confirmed;* and *for decisive measures* becomes *for such a decision.* Also, the section break that occurs five lines down from this paragraph is later omitted.

22. *those cushions:* becomes *those very cushions.*

23. *"Not—":* A question mark is added.

24. *"come nearer":* becomes *come nearer to me.*

25. *Vandergraves:* The phrase *last night* is added after this word.

26. *sick headache:* becomes simply *headache.* Also, the last two sentences become one, joined at *for her, I've already told you—."*

27. *"our talk that I've asked you to come up this afternoon"*: becomes *our talk of last night that I've asked you to come up."*

28. *"You must recognize that I know what's best for Tina"*: becomes *I suppose you'll admit that I know what's best for Tina."*

29. *in this room you asked me:* becomes *in this room, years ago, you asked me.*

30. *"But Charlotte"*: A comma is added between these words.

31. *"No, not all."*: A semicolon replaces the comma.

32. *Charlotte looked up with a glitter of apprehension in her eyes:* Charlotte's last name is added and *eyes* becomes *hunted eyes.*

33. *her purpose:* becomes *her tremendous purpose.* Also, *she said* becomes *she announced.*

34. *Charlotte stared:* Charlotte's last name is added.

35. *"Jim would have approved of that too."*: In this paragraph, *to my family* becomes *to the Lovells;* the dash after *Tina* becomes a period; *and why* begins a new sentence.

36. *whatever—might come of it?"*: In this paragraph, the comma is omitted after *child* and an additional *whatever* is added after the dash.

37. *"you—our leaving"*: The dash is replaced by a semicolon. Also, the section break that occurs here is later omitted.

38. *"your pride?"*: *she exclaimed* is added after this.

39. *Charlotte caught her up again:* becomes *Charlotte echoed the words with a desolate laugh.*

40. *"Yes—compassionately, as I used to love"*: The dash becomes a semicolon and the comma becomes a dash. Also, elsewhere in this paragraph, the comma in *Nonie, exactly* becomes a semicolon.

41. *everything—:* The dash becomes a semicolon.

42. *"You sacrifice"*: becomes *You do sacrifice.*

43. *laboring:* adopts the British spelling.

44. *hands was stirring:* becomes *arms was faintly stirring.*

CHAPTER XI

1. *so brief a betrothal:* During medieval times, the period of betrothal was entered into by a simple but solemn practice known as handfasting, during which the couple joined hands in front of witnesses and promised to wed at a future date. As simple as this custom appears, it was considered a legally binding contract. Traditionally, while the betrothal could last anywhere from a few weeks to several months, the period of a year and a day was common, for it encompassed the four seasons and thus symbolized that the couple's love was enduring and would last a lifetime. Also, in this paragraph, *in New York that* becomes *in the New York of those times;* the semicolon goes outside the quotation marks after *other; regarded as being also newly acquainted* becomes *regarded as being also newly known to each other; Southern* becomes lowercased; and *in the annals of Virginia and Maryland* becomes simply *in their annals.*

2. *her late husband's morals:* In this paragraph, *hardly surprising that tradition had been disregarded* becomes *it was no great surprise to anyone that tradition should have been disregarded;* the dash in *I—unless* becomes a semicolon; and *had her doing so appeared to "cast a slur" on her late husband's morals* becomes *if her doing so could have been construed as "casting a slur" on her late husband.*

3. *from the general inheritance:* In this paragraph, *black eyes* becomes *brown eyes; to be pronounced against her* becomes *to be needful; would have been an exaggeration* becomes *would be an exaggeration;* and *around* becomes *round.*

4. *they gradually desisted:* In this paragraph, the semicolon goes outside the quotation marks after *off; since Mrs. Manson Mingott had broken her husband's will, nothing like it had been seen in New York* becomes *since that dauntless woman, Mrs. Manson Mingott, had broken her husband's will, nothing like her attitude had been seen in New York; with epigram* becomes *by dint of epigram;* the exclamation point after *adoption* is preceded by a dash; and the comma after *wonder* is omitted.

5. *a risk must not be renewed:* In this paragraph, *her own bedroom mirror* becomes *Delia's own bedroom mirror; In those few hours* becomes *During those few days; Delia perceived* becomes *Delia discovered;* and *Charlotte's misgivings* becomes *Charlotte's fears.*

6. *perfect propriety of its arrangements:* In this paragraph, *precipitation which made it evident* becomes *precipitation which showed;* the dash in *marriage—though* becomes a semicolon; *would not admit such drawbacks* becomes *would not admit even to themselves that such drawbacks;* and *For* is omitted from the beginning of the last sentence.

7. *between them:* The period that ends this paragraph is replaced by an ellipsis.

8. *her own stifled youth:* In this paragraph, *endless* becomes *continual* and the conjunction *and* is added after *self-abasement* (the semicolon remains).

9. *on a sunlit torrent:* In this paragraph, *fact that* becomes *fact which; mamma* becomes capitalized; *she had whispered* becomes *Tina had whispered;* and the dashes that set off the clause *Delia, Charlotte, even the gallant Lanning* become commas.

10. *mean streets:* a reference to the physical quality of the streets: as the neighborhood is being developed, they are most likely still rough and difficult to navigate.

11. *narrows of Hell Gate:* Hell Gate—or, in Dutch, Helegat (Bright Passage)— is located at the confluence of the Harlem and East rivers. During Wharton's day it was a narrow passage with strong and erratic currents, as well as dangerous submerged rock ledges.

12. *Sheraton consoles and cabinets:* a design style named for its creator, cabinet-maker/publisher/preacher Thomas Sheraton (1751–1806). Such furniture boasted square, straight lines; round or slender legs that tapered to the foot; and highly ornate surfaces decorated with carvings, inlay, and even paintings.

13. *place must eventually be sold:* In this paragraph, *swept* becomes *bore,* the comma after *approached* is omitted, and *network* becomes hyphenated.

14. *pis aller:* French for *to go worse;* in other words, to worsen or the last expedient. Also, in this paragraph, *pis aller* becomes hyphenated and *Halseys discreetly favored* becomes *Halseys favoured.*

15. *cat-boat:* a single-masted sailboat with a broad beam.

16. *damask roses and mignonette:* The Lovell Place garden boasts exotic flowers. The red or pink damask roses are indigenous to Asia and possess a particularly sweet smell; from them, perfume oil is decocted. The dainty mignonette, a plant native to the Mediterranean, possesses small clusters of fragrant green flowers.

17. *orange-trees:* Perhaps because of their rarity or the care with which they had to be grown in colder climates (which would connote their fragility), orange blossoms were traditional wedding flowers in the nineteenth century.

18. *haycocks:* a British term describing rounded mounds of hay.

19. *Araby:* Further evidence that Lovell Place's garden boasts exotic scents: it is likened to Arabia, which is associated with heady, sensuous, intoxicating fragrances. Also, in this paragraph, *anyone's* becomes *any one's.*

20. *"India mull":* short for the obsolete Hindi term "mullmull," which refers to a soft, thin muslin material—hence, *India* mull.

21. *Brussels veil:* a veil made of Brussels lace, for which the city in Belgium is famous.

22. *pier-glass:* A pier is the space between two doors, windows, or archways. A pier-glass is thus the mirror which adorns this space and is often complemented by a pier-table.

23. *pier-glass would reflect tomorrow!:* In this paragraph, the semicolon after *empty* becomes a colon; *it had been a mistake* becomes *it had perhaps been a mistake; satin sandals* becomes *flat satin sandals; she had entered that same room* becomes *she had left that same room.*

24. *on two hundred plates:* becomes *on at least two hundred plates.*

25. *doylies:* usually *doily,* a small linen or lace placement or napkin. In this case, either meaning would be appropriate.

26. *"Yes. . . . . Thank you:* becomes *"Yes.—Thank you"*

27. *at her blunder:* The section break that occurs after this is omitted.

28. *for the morrow:* The comma that follows this phrase becomes a semicolon. Also, the section break that follows this paragraph is omitted.

29. *"possibly—":* The two single dashes become a single long dash.

30. *she falteringly ended:* Here, *agree with me that a word* becomes *agree with me, don't you, that a word,* and the comma after *time* becomes a question mark.

31. *reflection in the pier-glass:* In this paragraph, *answered abruptly* becomes simply *answered; in her the stirring* becomes *in her tone the stirring; should at times grow* becomes *should, at such times, grow; but she saw no reason why this change of mood should interfere with what she deemed to be her own duty* becomes *and in the*

present case she saw no reason why this change of mood should interfere with what she deemed to be her own duty; exchanges becomes singular; and *broad light* becomes *broad band of light.* Also, the section break that occurs after this paragraph is omitted.

32. *the glass above her shoulder:* In this paragraph, *faced each other* becomes *scrutinized each other,* and *glass* becomes *looking-glass.*

33. *"now—to speak":* The dash is omitted.

34. *"I thought—":* The dash becomes an ellipsis.

35. *"Not to?" Delia scrutinized her:* The question mark is omitted, and the paragraph begins *Delia looked at her cousin.* Elsewhere in the paragraph, *What mystery* becomes *What new mystery.*

36. *"I don't understand you, Charlotte":* The *you* is omitted. Additionally, the dash that ends this dialogue becomes an ellipsis.

37. *"which of us is her mother?":* becomes italicized.

38. *"Which of us?":* The question mark is preceded by a dash.

39. *"just tonight.":* In this paragraph, the comma in *calm, quite* becomes a semicolon, and the period that ends the dialogue becomes an ellipsis.

40. *rush of pity that always:* The *that* becomes *which.* Elsewhere, *feeling* becomes *sensation.*

41. *"it's been between us":* becomes *it's the word that's been between us.* Elsewhere in this paragraph, the comma after *good enough for you* becomes a semicolon, and a comma is added after *mercy.*

42. *smoldering:* changed to the British spelling. Also, the section break that occurs after this paragraph is omitted.

43. *first, hated:* The comma becomes a semicolon.

44. *envelope:* becomes *envelop.*

45. *"she should call you mother":* In this paragraph, *mother* becomes enclosed with single quotation marks (on both occasions); *she must never guess. But if you hadn't* becomes *she must never guess . . . but if you hadn't;* the *had* in *she'd have had to love me* becomes italicized; and the comma after *generosities* is omitted.

46. *murmured; and then,:* The *and* is omitted.

47. *Charlotte's feet on the stairs:* The section break that occurs here is omitted.

48. *that maternal passion: that* becomes *her.*

49. *Delia, her heart:* The comma is omitted. Elsewhere, the comma is omitted after *sacrilegious thing.*

50. *Delia stood up:* becomes *Delia rose.*

51. *"To think of something—something to say to her without—without her guessing.":* The dashes become ellipses, and the period becomes an ellipsis as well.

52. *she whispered suddenly: suddenly* is omitted.

53. *sky that filled: that* becomes *which.*

54. *good night:* becomes one word.

55. *Tina murmured:* becomes *Tina murmured through her dream.*

56. *"you darling!":* becomes *you darling mother!"*

READING GROUP GUIDE

1. Note the manner in which the author repeatedly describes rooms, furniture, and clothing. What sort of atmosphere is she attempting to evoke?

2. If *The Old Maid* were a drama, the significant male characters—Joe and Jim Ralston, Clement Spender, Lanning Halsey—would seem to have been purposely kept offstage. Why does Wharton do this? Some critics comment on Charlotte's failing to share the "blame" for Tina's birth with Clem Spender, choosing instead to accept the burden of her situation all alone, acting almost like a martyr. However, Charlotte did willingly have an affair with Spender. Do you think Charlotte is being unreasonable in her martyrdom? Do you think she is simply acting as the society of her day would expect her to act, or does she gain satisfaction from her selflessness?

3. Consider the repeated references to Delia's "ormolu clock represent[ing] a shepherdess" and a shepherd stealing a kiss from her. What significance does this clock play in the story? What is it meant to tell us about Delia's past, about her aspirations? Does this clock hold any special meaning for Charlotte?

4. Consider Edith Wharton as an author in the 1920s writing about the 1850s. Does she seem to be representing the era objectively, or commenting upon it? What meaning does the story have to twenty-first-century readers, who are even further removed than Wharton's audience was? Is *The Old Maid* simply a period piece, or does it have something to say even now?

5. When Delia derails Charlotte's marriage, Wharton, delving into Delia's thoughts, says: "Had she done right? Had she done wrong? And would she ever know?" Do you believe that Delia doesn't, at that moment, truly know her motivations, truly know whether she's done right or wrong? Why do you think that Wharton leaves the issue so open-ended?

6. *The Old Maid* explores the tragic results of a woman's acting on her sexual impulses, and details the so-called double standard, in which women are punished for actions no worse than what is deemed appropriate when men do them. And yet it is also a work in which two victimized women are locked in combat against each other. What, do you believe, is Wharton's stance on women's sexuality? And can this novel be read as a work of feminism?

A Note on the Type

The principal text of this Modern Library edition
was set in a digitized version of Janson, a typeface that
dates from about 1690 and was cut by Nicholas Kis,
a Hungarian working in Amsterdam. The original matrices have
survived and are held by the Stempel foundry in Germany.
Hermann Zapf redesigned some of the weights and sizes for
Stempel, basing his revisions on the original design.

MODERN LIBRARY IS ONLINE AT
WWW.MODERNLIBRARY.COM

MODERN LIBRARY ONLINE IS YOUR GUIDE TO CLASSIC LITERATURE ON THE WEB

THE MODERN LIBRARY E-NEWSLETTER

Our free e-mail newsletter is sent to subscribers, and features sample chapters, interviews with and essays by our authors, upcoming books, special promotions, announcements, and news.

To subscribe to the Modern Library e-newsletter, send a blank e-mail to: sub_modernlibrary@info.randomhouse.com or visit www.modernlibrary.com

THE MODERN LIBRARY WEBSITE

Check out the Modern Library website at www.modernlibrary.com for:

- The Modern Library e-newsletter
- A list of our current and upcoming titles and series
- Reading Group Guides and exclusive author spotlights
- Special features with information on the classics and other paperback series
- Excerpts from new releases and other titles
- A list of our e-books and information on where to buy them
- The Modern Library Editorial Board's 100 Best Novels and 100 Best Nonfiction Books of the Twentieth Century written in the English language
- News and announcements

Questions? E-mail us at modernlibrary@randomhouse.com
For questions about examination or desk copies, please visit the Random House Academic Resources site at www.randomhouse.com/academic